OWEN KARIUKI

F.R.E.D.

TEEN DETECTIVE

MISSING IN ACTION

F.RE.D. Teen Detective – Missing in Action

Published by Lee's Press and Publishing Company
www.LeesPress.net

This document is published by Lee's Press and Publishing Company located in the United States of America. It is protected by the United States Copyright Act, all applicable state laws and international copyright laws. The information in this document is accurate to the best of the ability of Owen Kariuki at the time of writing. The content of this document is subject to change without notice.

ISBN-13: 978-0997862379 *Paperback*
ISBN-10: 0997862378

Table of Contents

1

Left Out

And to think that this holiday would be the most boring ever," Jay Clarke, my best buddy, said, sighing lazily as he settled in the passenger seat of my Parson V200. "I almost started missing our job."

"Yuck," I replied, strapping on my seat belt. It was Saturday morning, and I felt as if Jay and I needed a little time out from our internship program with a local entrepreneurial company in town. It was a fun experience and worthwhile – but also tiring, and we needed some air to freshen up.

"So, where to, Fred?" Jay asked, giving me a wry look. "I hope you're not thinking of the library."

I laughed. Count on my friends to always cheer me up. Jolene Sanders, my other best friend, is equally funny but she was not available as she was going to catch up with us after having her skateboarding practices. "Since we're free for the weekend, and I don't expect Mr. Green to need our assistance, I propose the arcade," I said, driving down Berth Street.

"Oooh. Someone's naughty," Jay said with a sidelong look of sarcasm. "Anyway, how do you like the internship?" he asked, changing the topic.

"I'm impressed that Mr. Green found favor in our applications. Although posting me as a clean-up kid didn't strike my fancy at all," I said.

"Try a janitor's faggot," Jay added, sticking his tongue out. "But, it's worth it since I have a lot of access to the building. Greens Association is very state-of-the-art. You should visit the Resource Center – it is equipped with hi-tech PC's, an enormous library, and it even has a gallery full of scientific equipment."

I nodded. "I wish Jolene had some time to spare, and we could take her there." As I steered the car onto the main highway, my mind wandered to the serene ambiance of the summer morning. The sun was shining immaculately, thawing the atmosphere slowly. I knew it was going to get a bit shimmery during the day, but this condition was awesomely wonderful. My thoughts were intercepted by Jay's phone chime, "Who is it?"

Jay fished out his sleek phone, and immediately a dark frown took over his face. "A private number," he whispered. "Who would use a private number to contact me?"

I was afraid Jay was overreacting until he flashed his phone's screen at me with a hint of annoyance.

"You see?" he asked, shaking his head gloomily. "Maybe it is Mr. Green," I supplied. Even though that option sounded very far-fetched, *still...*

I was willing my mind to stop and think that maybe it was one of those phone hackers who was used to pranking oblivious people with fake calls, blank text messages, or oblique photos.

Jay shot me an anxious look through his olive eyes and shrugged. "I just don't picture someone as designated and distinguished as Mr. Green stooping so low as to," he stopped in mid-word as his attention shifted to the call. "Um…Hello? Who's this?"

As Jay spoke to his anonymous caller, I turned off the Walt Street exit and rode left headed for the too-conspicuous arcade center. The streets were teen-infested, none of them barely giving attention to the cars which slowly dragged through the packed road. Surprised that many guys would be interested in coming to the arcade; I found a spot at the sidewall of the arcade building; a two-story plaza with flashing lights inside, neon billboards all over the frontage, and an attractive ad posted at the door.

If I wasn't wrong, it seemed most of the kids were crowded around the splashy advert in a frenzy. Some were screaming in delight, holding their cameras and clicking away at the poster, probably being overwhelmed by the possibility that it would mean much to them when the picture was on a camera. Three lean guys who looked like college material huddled below the poster, well below it, I could make out what was on it to get a picture taken.

Jay tapped me on the shoulder, twirled his finger near his temple, and pointed at his phone. *Okay, the caller is crazy?* He hung up desperately and stashed his phone inside his jeans pocket roughly.

"Who was it?" I blurted out, sounding overly curious that Jay gave me a shake of his head. "Sorry, it's just that I was wondering what exactly is going on out here. I've never seen such a large crowd of kids gathered in one place at the same time before."

"Aaah!" Jay shook his head again, this time in bewilderment as we walked towards the arcade's flocked entrance. "It was just a wacko who wouldn't gain the temerity to even speak back. We both were as silent as brick. I almost began to think it was…"

He broke off. Not because he was cut short by anything serious, but because a very rowdy dude with sunglasses, curly hair, and skinny ripped jeans began to blabber like a timed human chatter-box, hunched over the wall and smiling to himself. I already disliked this guy even before what he was saying had made sense to Jay or me.

"This is the *craziest* thing in the world. Not only is the science convention free and totally *not* inclusive, but the invitations came via phone!" He grabbed his phone with a lot of zeal and waved it around some equally enthralled kids.

"What does he mean? A science convention?" Jay asked skeptically.

"Invites coming by phone?" I added, scratching a spot in my hair.

"You've got to be kidding, dude," the rowdy kid nosed in, slapping my shoulder too hard. His brown hair hid the mischievous look that spilled from his dark eyes and he had a lot of jewelry hanging from his neck, fingers, and wrists to his cheeks – stubs, obviously. "Haven't you gotten any blank messages, free videos or private number calls?" he asked arrogantly.

"Well, *I* have," Jay spoke up, still reeling from the blow of the whole situation. "Just now, I received a disturbing anonymous phone call. Is that supposed to be an invite to a science convention and not a sick prank?"

The kid nodded emphatically and waved his phone at Jay's face. "Seems like you are among one of the few lucky people chosen to attend *that* famous scientist's science convention. How awesome!" He crooned, pointing at the poster that was now surrounded by some enthusiastic nerdy types wooing at the face of a tough-looking, blue-eyed blond man.

I sealed my lips tight as a bleak realization dawned on me. I didn't want Rowdy Kid here to know about it, so after he sauntered away I urged Jay closer and said, "Maybe this is just a phone hacker trying to play with you, Jay?"

He drew back in repulse, crunched up his face into a grimace and furled his hands across his puffed-up chest.

"Really, Fred? Well, what a convenient time to bring that up. You know, it sounds like you're plain jealous," he growled, narrowing his eyes at me weirdly.

"Jealous of?" I pressed.

"You didn't get any blank text, call or even a video or photo, so that means *you* didn't get invited!" Jay spat, a disturbed look crossing his eyes. "Hey, you know that sounds rather odd, Fred."

I smiled, glad that Jay had decided to rid the lame excuse that I was jealous and concentrate on less trivial matters. "I've heard about phone hackers using such methods to fool around with people but now that almost every kid here's got the same call, then that definitely rules out that theory," I said, suddenly feeling left out. "But why haven't I gotten the call?"

"P-lease! I mean, you can never be *so* sure." Jay reached for my phone before I could check and flipped it on. He scrolled through my unread texts and call log and then sighed deeply, handing me the phone. "I'll take that back."

I shrugged, reading through my texts in despair. None seemed to have been sent by any anonymous person, in fact, Jolene had sent me a text reading 'Just finished practices.

Meet you at... lemme guess the arcade! Have some weird guy calling me with a private number.'

"Oh, even Jolene got the invite," I moaned, texting her back; 'Nice guess, btw. Bu-bye.' Turning to Jay with a grievous expression in my eyes, I said, "Do you really believe this? A famous scientist in town, launching a science convention, and I miss out?"

Jay shook his head dismally. "It's sad; Fred, but you can take my invite anyway. I'm not that much of a science buff." He fumbled for his phone from his pocket and proffered it to me, wriggling his eyebrows menacingly. "I'll bet you'll have so much fun. You deserve it as you got an A in that science pop quiz last term; and maintaining *or* getting an A is pretty hard."

Just then, the door to the arcade was pulled open by a beefy plump guy; with a crispy crew-cut and a bulgy nose that resembled a mini-sized sumo-wrestler. His exaggerated smile quickly drew the kids closer to him.

"Hi, kids. I see you all got the invites to Mr. Gerald Kruger's science convention, huh" he said, wringing his hands gleefully.

Rowdy Kid, whom I came to learn that his real name was Danson McHale; bobbed up and down in sheer ecstasy as if he were about to explode intominuscule pieces of annoying over-excited Danson McHales. "Of course, No wonder we're here. I, personally, am a big fan of...um, what's the guy's name again?"

The beefy guy chuckled. "Gerald Kruger, famous aeronautical engineer; and also, the maker of the first prototype of a…" The guy's smile faded once he noticed the unwanted publicity he was getting from onlookers. He smiled back shyly at the kids. "I guess I'll have to tell you all this *inside*. That's for those who have the invites."

My heart dropped like a metal plunger. It was, for sure, heartbreaking to watch the kids proceed inside the arcade while flashing their phones at the beefy man who would nod satisfactorily and usher them in. Why wasn't I among them? Oh, I knew that perfectly well.

Jay walked tentatively toward the heavy-set man who gave me the most haunting look, turned briefly to me at the empty pavement, and mouthed a *Sorry* before walking in; and the door swinging back and shutting with a sickening thud.

2

Out of Place

As hard as I tried to put on a frigid expression on my face, I couldn't help but feel a stab of pain in my heart. Frankly, it was not because Jay had decided to go without me, (obviously, I lacked an invite, or missed to get one!) but it was the mere reason that my wish of going to the convention had been put out so sadly. I brought my phone up to my face and stared at the screen for a very long time, maybe waiting for the call or text to come through.

After trial and error, I gave up and walked to my car. It is better if I don't think about it right now, I told myself, as I pulled out from the alley. Inches away from the block, the car gave a violent jolt and grumbled. I pounded on the gas pedal constantly, but my precious Parson was *out of gas*! My eyes wandered from the green LED on the gas gauge to the sudden bright light that filtered through the rectangular outline of a side door to the arcade.

"Out of luck this time," I mumbled; as I jumped out of the car and began dragging it to the curb. It took me some minutes to get it to realign with the well-marked white tracks that showed the parking spaces. Checking to ensure I had my phone with me, just in case the caller found me busy, I ran to the side door.

I was not in the least worried whether the door was open or locked since I had a trusty bobby pin. I know, I sound like I'm always prepared to do things such as breaking into places often, huh? See, being an amateur detective requires you always to believe a crime is in the making. I'm not saying that my failing to get invited to Mr. Kruger's science convention had to have been planned, no! But, just the thought that Jay was in there, and he probably knew how to kick butt and not look for anything fishy, made me squirm. So, in one way or the other, I was fine with leaving my car hungry for some petrol, intentionally of course, to buy time.

This door was *bolted* on the *inside*. The only way I would enter was to run into it, drawing too much attention of the bystanders or pedestrians who were teeming around; and also to the beefy inspector-guy.

I scanned the four-meter wall which was slightly curvilinear at the top. There was no ladder that ran to the top of it, and neither was there a vent or a hatch. I knew the arcade quite well, and this was typical of it so; I should have known better than to try and sneak in. Wasn't there even a security guard around?

"Hey, whatcha doing?" a voice, positively feminine, called out.

I jerked back, stuffing the bobby pin somewhere between my blond hair locks and smiling nervously. At Jolene. "Um…just sight-seeing. I've never gotten much used to this city."

"Save it, Fred," Jolene said; chuckling and leaning on her legendary roguish-looking skateboard. Her copper-brown hair had been pushed under a pink sisal sunhat, revealing her tanned face, blue eyes; and a smirk on her cherry lips. "I know you *a lot*. And there's no way you haven't gotten much of Glades because you've lived here practically forever."

The way she stressed on 'a lot' made me shiver; but in a good way. I sighed, walking her to the curb. "I wasn't breaking and entering so; I'm not guilty of anything." I nodded at her phone which was always either in her pocket or palm; and explained to her all about the invite, the convention and not forgetting the fact that I hadn't gotten one.

"Is that bad?" Jolene asked bluntly.

I rolled my eyes as she giggled. "I know it sounds as if I'm envious of you and Jay getting invited, but it's totally in good faith." I gulped. Yeah right. "Jay and every other kid who got invited are in the arcade. Some brawny guy is taking them through the arcade before the convention starts at...hmm, precisely an hour from now."

Jolene shook her head sadly and touched my shoulder. "As a friend, I'm willing to give you my invite. I'm not a sciency chick," she said with a long frown. "You got an A on that science test, didn't you? Mr. Rinaldi was very pleased with you. I don't see why you shouldn't go."

"Jay did and said the same thing, but I am a real friend and wouldn't take advantage of you," I countered, shrugging. "Anyway, it looks like you and Jay are going to have fun because the convention is being held at your second-best spot in town."

"The mall?" Jolene spurted out in disgust.

"Stop with the sarcasm, Jo," I said; turning to my car. "I have to go and refuel my car. The gas is over and it's not like I intentionally felt that it needed a limited amount so that I'd do something else as I waited for the gas man to come by and give me credit." I smiled nervously. "No way. I'm not that weird!"

Jolene bid me good-bye and gave me a confused look as she walked in the arcade. I also found it weird not refilling my fuel at convenient times and leaving the car to drag itself with less gas. Finally, I'd run into a gas station and relieve my car of such misery, but at least I get a discount on gas. Guess I'm just weird in my own small way. So much that I even failed to get an invite to a science convention!

Darren Thompsons, the local mechanic, wasn't really impressed with my forgetting to refuel my tank again. "Are you *that* desperate for the discount offer?" he had asked, handing me the cans of kerosene from the back of his truck.

"WOW! Darren that would be very underhanded of me," I had bluffed.

"I just wanted to refresh the tank fully."

Darren smiled a knowing smile. He had been a personal savior to me whenever my car ran out of gas, not intentionally but accidentally, so he knew very well I was bluffing. "You intentionally want credit, Fred. I know that. But you should make sure that you fill up your tank regularly; or else your car will begin failing. You never know."

I had shaken my head. Who knew my corrupt little way to get credit from Darren would end up having such effects to my car? "Okay, Darren. Guilty as charged. I'll turn a new leaf now."

As I drove home, I was only relieved that he hadn't actually renounced giving me credits.

The street where we lived, Tall Street, is usually very lively and the residents are quite warm, cordial, fun; and sociable. Be it the noises from the neighbors' kids, loud ear-harrying music, barking from agitated dogs, or cars zooming back and forth; there's always some sort of activity taking place. However, I was feeling out of place as my car rolled past every house. It was creepily silent, except for the rustle of leaves and the tree fronds thrashing against each other in a symphony of crunching branches.

"Whoa! Is it me, or is it suddenly very quiet?" I didn't want to answer myself as it was very overwhelming to think that everyone was...*gone*.

I quickly slid my car, now full of gas, but without any credit to the driver; into our driveway and bounced out, raring to know whether Dad and Mom were in. Practically, it seemed they weren't around, explaining the fact that the garage was empty. Dad's taken Mom for lunch, I thought grimly. Not that I didn't like that guess.

My senses were telling me that there was someone roaming inside my house, but I wasn't 100% sure. A blurry figure was standing close to the bay window, fumbling with the mauve curtain, giving me more than 100% surety that we had an unwanted visitor. Squatting beside the wall, I advanced slowly towards the door, copped hold of the rather sweaty doorknob (maybe it was my hands) and wrenched it open.

"AAAH!" a wimpy scream emanated from whoever was standing behind the curtain.

I had to admit I was a little bit freaked out, but it looked like whoever had screamed wasn't really skilled at subtlety or screaming as well. As I neared the curtain, I noted the black hair, tall build, and the high-maintenance oxfords of a familiar person jutting from beneath and knew to the max that it must have been...

"Roy Watson!" I blurted, shoving aside the curtain and gasping "What's my long-time, nerve-wrecking, nemesis doing in my house?"

3
Knock, Knock...Disaster

Do you have to rub it all in, Fred?" Roy barked back, clearly looking offended and off-guard.

Just by the fact that Roy Watson, the not-so-friendly nag in my life, had been lingering around my house; made a chill run down my spine. He was, nevertheless, not close to remorseful and was brushing off the dust from his sparkly turquoise suit and well-styled hair.

"Are you always that *formal*?" I asked, looking surprised.

Roy didn't crack a smile, but his eyes flickered with pride. *That goon!* "Fred, Fred, Fred, you never cease to bore me! Apparently, since you act like some weird inquisitor, I'm gonna say that I landed a cool job as a PR manager for a famous scientist who's in town," Roy said, flipping his long coat and glancing down at his oxfords. "Seemingly, I can relate very well with puppies, oh, I mean *people*."

Gritting my teeth, I brushed past Roy and began looking around the lounge and kitchen.

"What are you doing now, Fred?" Roy sneered, folding his arms in a so-not-cool way.

"Just checking whether anything's gone missing. I don't mean to be snippy, Roy. It's just that with you here; I fear you'd have a more sinister motive."

Roy shrugged. "As a matter of fact, yes, I did have a sinister motive being here, Fred," he said with a revealing look. Partly I didn't like that look, but it meant more than just trying to piss me off. Did he have anything to hide?

"What?" I tried to sound like a thrilled cheerleader getting her first leap.

Roy reached for what looked like a mini-briefcase, set it on a coffee table; and zipped it open. I couldn't help but to move closer to take a look. "Oooh, Mr. Faux Detective is finally interested," he cooed, chuckling forcibly. Inside, he dug for a folder stuck between reams of paper and handed it to me. "I believe you'll be convinced or better; persuaded that I am here for a legit reason," he added smugly.

I hated this guy! Staring at the folder like it contained fairy dust; I slowly opened it and turned it over. Some off-white papers flew out and landed on my lap. It wasn't really the best thing to think, but maybe this time Roy was close to convincing me. Where had he found these documents? Or, where had he *stolen* these documents from? One document particularly read that Roy Watson was free to sell Gerald Kruger's work to his prospective market and even officiate at the opening of the convention.

Turning a look of disbelief at Roy, I slowly said, "Really? You, PR?"

Roy nodded, almost as if he wasn't ready for that reaction. He snatched the document and rolled them into the folder. "Now, I guess you know the reason *why* I was here, Fred. It's self-explanatory and not debatable."

I had not known such a thing was in the offing, so I was pretty taken aback. But clearly, Roy was missing one point. "You were trespassing, Roy. And I'm willing to bet that's not supposed to be good work ethics, huh?" I said, smirking.

"Don't you get it? I am here to invite you to the science convention, Fred; officially. . It's your lucky day," Roy declared, widening his arms and embracing me, amid some struggle. He pulled back, straightened his suit and cleared his voice. "Sorry for that. I know it's been hard for you, Fred. For such a low-profile and a lowly little shrewd kid, you really have it tough sometimes, don't you?"

I gave him a shocked look. Roy was getting on my nerves, insult by insult. "How did you know I needed an invitation?" I asked simply. "Did you know I hadn't been invited?" Roy chuckled uneasily then tugged at his bowtie. "Um...um..." And now he was mumbling. "I...I...am...just being a great friend to you; trying to save you from impending shame and embarrassment. So, are you going to question the hand that giveth or just take what it giveth?"

"OK. First, friend? Second, you're really not good with the old version of English," I said. "And thirdly, you *have* to tell me how you got to know this. This is big. I mean, Roy Watson hasn't always that much of a philanthropist."

"Tell me about it," Roy groused under his breath, and then he sighed. "I'm not hiding anything, and you should learn to accept gifts from your nemesis once in a while." He held his hand out to me and gave me a card that looked like a debit card, but with a profile pictogram of Kruger imprinted on it.

"How did you?"

Roy held up his hand. "Just accept it without having to painfully interrogate me," he said, still frowning. He reached for the front door and momentarily glared back at me. "Oh, and this is *not* a favor." As soon as Roy left, the house became silent again. But instead on concentrating on the tranquility, my mind was already surfing on a web of confusion. I decided to call Jay. It was already show-time, and I figured it would be good if he acted like my; 'I spy with my little eye' guy. Not that I didn't trust the card Roy had given me. (Okay, I did).

Jay answered on the third ring. "Hi, Fred. It's so unfortunate you're not here. The convention is actually going to be launched here at the arcade, and the venue will be at the Marino Grounds. Festive, isn't it?" he said.

"Actually Jay, I'm kinda in need of your help here." I clued him in on Roy's sudden run-in, the odd invitation, and everyone being somehow *gone*. "Is all that sensible?" I asked.

I heard Jay's dry cackle from the other end of the line. He better not think I'm still jealous, I thought. "Well, there are a lot of guys in here, so maybe everyone left to come for the convention. We even have teen celebrity Fred Guzzle, and he's not just cool because he shares a name with you."

"Stick to the point," I instructed him coolly.

"Okay, Fred. Roy being at your house at this time when almost everyone is here *being* strange…unless he never got the invite too."

"He's the PR rep for the occasion, Jay. I don't see why he needs an invite."

Jay's repeated laughs almost made my eardrums pop.

"Yeah, I had also meant to laugh; but not until he showed me his contract and some documents legalizing his job as a PR," I said. "That guy is unbelievable."

"You got that right bro," Jay said, amid some rocking beats of a classical song over the stereo. "So, he was at your house all alone, gave you a tangible invite, said he's a PR, showed you some documents; and even *hugged* you? Bro, that's so twisted! I think it's a ploy."

"I thought the same after I saw the fake-looking cheap paper material of the document. It looked like…like some grainy material."

"Well, that seems made-up. But why would Roy do that? He isn't a criminal," Jay said. "At heart, he may be. But he's not that devious and fraudulent."

I bit my lip. Crazy thoughts began whirling around my cloudy mind. Roy wearing a black costume and sneaking into my home, already armored with a pre-planned excuse, stealing or doing something less of him; then succeeding by getting me to believe him. Hmmm, sounds like him but…

"I know, but he knew that I hadn't been invited; which makes him liable of having been linked with my failing to come to the convention," I reasoned out loud. "What do you think Jay?"

Jay sighed and then spoke up, "I just think the two of us are taking this way too far." He paused briefly as the background music died out. "Oh, Fred, it's time! I have to go. I promise I'll text you whenever something suspicious happens."

"Okay. Thanks a lot, Jay." I hung up and smiled. How did I end up making him a whole lot like me?

Shifting my attention to the card that Mr. PR (for Pathetic Roy) had given me, I got a rush of puzzlement through my frosty body. I was beginning to shiver because Roy might have been faking it all this time.

The card looked very genuine, with my name on it; and the word PASS on it. But, why did I have second thoughts about it? The invites had to be via phone, not delivered personally. The more I thought about it, the more it came to light that Roy was beginning to do me more than just a favor.

An hour later, my tired feet were reclined on a hassock, my arms outstretched holding a smoothie glass and a mini-fan, my entire torso enjoying the sun's scorching rays, and my mind went into a lapse of relaxation over at Madame Cassandra's Hangout. *Sweet sweet sun*, I said, holding my head up to soak all the Vitamin D I desired, and that meant when I began to feel like a BBQ on a grill.

I was really having a nice time not worrying about the convention or Roy. The Hangout is the vent to my worries in life, and so, I couldn't afford to lose touch with the soothing inner peace that was offered for free within just four solid walls.

As I walked past a shelf of a collection of vintage tapes, I saw a very familiar man who was angrily railing at a scared-looking attendant; and pointing down at the tape he'd just picked right from the display. He then turned away and began storming out when he stopped abruptly at the doors. His head cocked backward, his steely eyes bulged out, and his flinty look remaining unreadable.

Afraid that he'd seen me eyeing him, I turned to face the shelf again, this time not looking too showy.

The man sauntered towards the attendant and began fondling her hands. ODE, I thought, feeling disgusted. Relieved that he was preoccupied, I moved to the next aisle of tapes and busied myself, blindly looking at the cover pictures of the tapes and placing them in their initial spots.

The man quickly spotted me, and this time, I swore that the look from his eyes was of sheer animosity; like he wasn't really comfortable with my presence.

As I drew my attention to the tapes, my phone rang, and I picked up Jolene's call without hesitation. "Hey, Jo. What's up?"

Her tone was that of distress. "You won't believe this, Fred, but our host Gerald Kruger is nowhere to be seen. Calls at his apartment are being intercepted by an anonymous caller, the police say. His fiancée has no idea about his whereabouts. In short, we've searched everywhere, but we can't find him!"

A few seconds later a message came through on my phone from an anonymous person.

If I Were You, I'd Be Happy I Never Got Invited!

4

Here We Go Again

I bolted out of the Hangout like a scalded dog. After informing Jolene that I was on my way, I got in my car and peeled away. The roads were clear, so I had an easy time getting to the arcade and in time too.

The moment I parked the car, Jay and Jolene hurriedly bolted out of the arcade and headed towards me. Their faces were pale and expressing worry.

"What happened guys? Is anyone hurt?" I asked, heaving rapidly. I'm really not good with missing people scenarios.

Jay was the first to regain his composure. "At least we aren't but Gerald is."

My eyes darted to the arcade door where a number of distraught parents were busy consoling their terrified kids. "Was it that bad?" I asked, beside myself with worry.

"The police aren't sure about Gerald going AWOL, but they presume it was a case of kidnap," Jolene said. "According to Officer Timmons, Gerald didn't even show up, which makes sense because we didn't see him during the launch."

I gulped, afraid that this was another undeniable case for me to solve.

"Well, let's start from scratch. The launch was due to start at one pm, and the convention was to start at three pm. In two hours Gerald would have made it, even if not punctually," I said.

"Do we have any suspects?" Jolene asked.

My mind was already churning. "Roy *has* been acting weird. He might be our first suspect," I supplied. Jay had already told Jolene about Roy and his over-the-top behavior.

"Believe me, Fred; Roy *could* hurt a fly or a bug or a fly-bug, but not Gerald. He's the PR manager for Goodness Sake! What motive could he have?" Jay asked, sounding skeptical.

"I say, for now, we try and focus on him," Jolene added. Her face then creased. "Fred, can I see that pass card that Roy gave you?" she asked.

I handed the card to her and then gave her a dubious look. If anything, she looked as if she wanted to double over with laughter; and at the same time gnaw at it to ensure it was genuine. "Roy must have lied to me. He gave me a worthless and useless card all for the sake of mockery. That jerk!"

"Perhaps he did it *for someone*," Jay said thoughtfully.

My body got all tingly. For certain, Jay was meaningful about it. It had not struck me earlier, but now I could see the certainty in it. But was Roy still capable of running such a plot on behalf of somebody?

Jolene cut into my thoughts suddenly. She was glancing down at my pass card with a look of contempt. "As much as you'd consider Roy to be a heinous criminal, perhaps you'd like to know that this pass card is not a fake," she said, shaking her head in disapproval.

"*What?*" Jay and I whooped in surprise.

Before Jolene could do any further explanation, Officer Timmons, the undoubtedly bulky inspector in charge of GPD; who had a handlebar mustache, unevenly cropped hair, and a nose the size of a hypodermic needle rushed by with a gang of younger-looking police. He was flushed, in a hurry to deliver whatever pressing news he had. Ever since I became an amateur detective and showed interest in solving crimes; the GPD have been my closest confidants, besides Jay and Jolene.

"Hello, Officer Timmons. What's the rush for?" I asked.

Clearly, his florid face and rolled up sleeves spelled way too much hastiness for the forty-five-year old guy. "Fred Turner, it's a relief you're here. I have to admit we really need your help. No one's best suited for this job than you," he breathed, gripping my shoulders with his iron palms.

Taken aback, I chuckled, "I'm game. What's up?"

"I know you've heard about Gerald; sad story for such a fresh mind.

So, I did all I can and sadly it seems to me that we have some clues we'd like to share with you *privately*," he insisted.

I followed him and the other cops into the squad car that was parked close, and I jumped in. Lined on the back seat, with logos of a certain company in town, were cartons and cardboard boxes which looked all mangled and wrecked. "What are these, Officer Timmons?" I asked.

"These are the boxes containing the different scientific products that a company in town, Greens Association, sells," Mr. Timmons explained. "Apparently, and ironically, they have a connection to the case."

I did a double take. Greens Association was where I did my internship for the summer! If it was linked to Gerald's kidnapping, boy was I ready to drop out with immediate effect. I didn't want Officer Timmons to know that so I kept it cool. "How so?"

"Well, when we tried calling Gerald's apartment in Laden Hill, some funny guy with a distorted speech said; we were never going to see Gerald again unless he pays up for something he cost him," Officer Timmons went on. "On asking what it was, he said we had to go to the apartment and see for ourselves. He said it was for the betterment of Gerald and Greens Association."

"So, you found these boxes at Gerald's apartment?" I presumed.

Officer Timmons gave me a short nod. He told one of the officers to hand him one of the boxes which turned out to contain some crushed pieces of electronic tweezers. "That is just one of the exhibits," he said, pushing more boxes aside. He heaved one onto his lap and pulled the flaps open. Inside was an expensive-looking phone which was now a meaningless ball of scrap metal.

"No," I said in disbelief, feeling the burn. Lucky, I had my phone still intact. "Who did this?"

"We don't know, for now. But, we think that Gerald might have done this, and that's why our anonymous guy said he had to pay for it," Officer Timmons said.

I shrugged. The thought of a renowned scientist marring the repute of Greens Association just before a convention; his hosting was wild and out of the picture. Wouldn't that instead mar his repute? I turned a skeptical brow at Officer Timmons. "Are you positive about this?"

"No," he said sadly; and then gave me a sincere look. "That's why we need you, Fred."

Glancing over at Jay and Jolene, they were talking to some kids about the incident, I was sure they'd accept to investigate this case. "As I said, I'm game," I said with finality.

The next few minutes we exchanged ideas and clues with Officer Timmons about Roy, and he promised to back me up with officers to check on Roy and my so-called invite. Even though Jolene hadn't told me why she thought it was a genuine favor, I was still convinced there was more to it than just that. Thanking him, I felt like a burden had been lifted off my back. Now, I had the big guns on *my* side. Cool!

I walked up to Jay and Jolene, and we discussed everything, including the offer that Officer Timmons had generously given to me.

"I think that's a great thing for you. You'll finally get to put your detective skills to work," Jolene said. Her face took a grave expression at once. "About your pass card, I had some tech guy from Smart Stores check for me just now, and he said it was completely genuine," she verified, handing me the card

I winced. "That means Roy was not plotting against me," I said.

"No surprise there," Jay added begrudgingly. "So, this throws this case off to another direction. What about Gerald?"

"Well," I said, walking them through the arcade door; I didn't need a pass for that. "Let's start clue-searching."

With bright and glowing lights fixed in the expansive walls, the arcade only needed a talented pyrotechnic to make it look like the fourth of July. Attractive banners and streamers were hanging all over the vaulted ceiling, reflecting the festive purple and red colors. A Mega Plasma TV had been set up on an upholstered wooden platform in which the Virtual DJ Pro program was mixing jumpy tunes and bouncy techno jams. It was like a dome full of the latest technological discoveries – there was blinding fog streaming at the stage which filled the arcade with a misty condition.

I could see some police officers busy questioning innocent kids, but I couldn't find the beefy guy anywhere. It would be very awkward if they failed to question that guy since he struck me as very suspicious.

"What's the plan, Fred?" Jay asked, plainly put off by the noises from outside. Evidently, the convention was gaining a lot of unwanted publicity.

Tumbling all sorts of ideas in my mind, I said, "You try and sniff out Roy, Jolene secure the perimeter, and I will take care of a sneaky character."

"You mean that kid McHale?" Jolene asked, frowning. "I think he has a *crush* on me. Weird kid he is, you bet. He kept giving me winks and air kisses."

Jay smiled mischievously as he punched Jolene on her forearm.

"Well, I guess you two are perfect for each other!"

We parted, and I decided to mooch around the stage. The stage fog and the bright lights gave it a mystical kaleidoscopic effect. Gerald must be a hustler, I thought. I would have thought he had rented the arcade for the launch, and so it seemed. I hadn't heard of Gerald Kruger actually, but he seemed to be very insecure to have been kidnapped on his big day.

I lingered around the raised platform and began scouring the arcade. Some seats and tables had been pushed away from the center of the gaming hall where the stereo had been set up. To accommodate the seats, the vending machines had been lugged all the way to a makeshift storage unit. It seems he really was anticipating, I figured. Then something struck me. There was one thing I had forgotten to check: the side-door!

"Side-doors really should be made accessible these days," I told myself as I slid behind the stage curtain.

I walked down a tiny flight of stairs that led to a narrow hallway flanked by whitewashed walls. There was blinding light at the other end which meant that the door was open. Smiling in satisfaction, I began walking towards it when I heard some weird tapping. Spinning to my heels, I began running headed to the other side when I saw a bulky figure barreling toward me, arms outstretched.

I turned and made it to the stage. Huffing, I looked around and spotted Officer Timmons standing at the entrance door, staring down at his notepad. He looked very calm until I came to him.

"Um…Officer Timmons, you've got to know this…" My words trailed off faintly.

"I beg to differ, Fred," Officer Timmons cut in with a tone of urgency. "This is more pressing. We think Roy Watson might have gone missing as well."

5

Clue Storming

What happened?" I asked, flustered.

Officer Timmons was already pacing out of the arcade in a frantic mood. His gray-brown hair; which usually peeked from under a worn out blue cap was now straggled around his apple face, concealing the beads of perspiration on his flat forehead. I could see this case taking a toll on him.

"A search conducted by some of our guys at his neighborhood revealed a rather disturbing confession from a nearby resident who believes he saw a guy dragging away a cheesy and snappy kid' whom I believe it *must* be Roy," Officer T said; giving me a wink and a weak smile. "That's kind of dangerous having two people already missing."

"Does it mean we're retrogressing?" I asked in disappointment.

"No. Just that the criminal is progressing faster than we are," Officer Timmons corrected, nibbling at his fingers. "I think we need a plan, Fred. This guy is striking with a lot of unexpected moves."

"Well, let's do a stakeout. They always work."

"On who? We have no suspects, Fred."

I remembered the guy I'd met at Hangout earlier and felt he was not very straight. You know what I mean. Before telling Officer Timmons, I made it clear to myself of how overshadowing Officer T could become when it came to handling cases. Maybe this was my time to also do a little snooping around. The mere fact that he'd not even let me report a case of a man chasing me back at the stage, (Now I bet he was long gone), made me think he was hogging the case too much.

"I'll just work something up with Jay and Jolene," I said, feeling guilty that I was forsaking Officer T after he'd helped me through to this point, so I added quickly; "But you could still look around and inform me of any signs of Gerald and Roy."

He shrugged plaintively and opened the door to his squad car. "I suppose that'd be better. I see you need some time to sort all this out," he said with no tinge of hurt. "I'll call you later. Please take care."

"I will." I watched as his squad car roared noisily and sped to the gnarly traffic-clogged downtown area. It felt as if I'd treated him inconsiderately, but then, I did need some time to get things set straight. My nemesis had just been kidnapped, and for the first time, I was *feeling* for Roy Watson. I was thinking of how belligerent he must have been when he was dragged away. Wow, I was beginning to miss him!

Jay and Jolene walked up to me as I was headed for my car. They looked wearied by all the sleuthing, and we decided to drop by Diner's Delight for lunch. It was close to two pm, one hour after the launch had begun; and disaster had struck.

After telling them of Roy's disappearance, the reactions I got were very...*expected.*

"I always had a premonition that that guy would get into trouble one day for being so rude, crude, and depraved;" Jay admitted from the passenger seat.

"For me, I bet Roy got what he wanted," Jolene said, folding her arms across her chest tightly. Her lips were drawn in a taut lip of contempt. "He is the PR manager, and now that the convention seems to be heading on a downhill, he's not doing good marketing."

"You think, that's why he was kidnapped...maybe by the same dude who kidnapped Gerald?" I asked.

"Not necessarily, but it could be a lead," Jolene said. "Look, Roy gives you a pass card which only he knows what its use is, then he gets kidnapped. Don't you see a connection?"

A connection? I wasn't viewing this the same way Jolene was, but she seemed to be making sense when she said there was a connection. Up until now, Roy was not guilty of anything, and now some random mugger had just abducted him which made it look like Roy had been kidnapped for a reason. For something he'd done.

I gave the blue pass card another glance and then back to the rushing white stripes on the road.

"Guys, I have a feeling the pass card did it," I said, steering around a sharp bend.

"What do you mean?" Jay asked doubtfully.

"It will only make sense somehow if we find the use of this card," I said. "Roy had a reason for giving me this card, and I know it was not because I lacked an invite. He may have known I hadn't been invited, but I honestly don't want to believe this pass is an invite. He had a concrete reason for giving it to me."

"But how did he know you needed it?" Jay was still not ready to believe.

"I don't know," I said as I pulled in front of Diner's Delight imposing a quaint façade, "but what I do know is that I'm starving."

We all paused a few seconds, glanced at each other and then yelled, "Pizza!"

About an hour after having lunch with Jay and Jolene at our favorite pizzeria; which serves low-cal pizzas with a very thin topping of macaroni and Big Macs, and dropping them at their homes, I decided to drive to Gerald's apartment. Actually, from Officer Timmons, it was a snug love nest for Gerald and his fiancée. Part of my senses was telling me it was just hot air, but the minute I was directed by the landlord, who seemed pretty disturbed by the news of his disappearance, I was ready to do anything but disagree.

It was an airy, bright, and spacious place with a lot of accessories that filled the shelves facing off the fireplace. All sorts of science-related tech stuff such as; gadgets, latest phone models, and even PC's and laptops were neatly arranged on a separate shelf. A fluffy red wall-to-wall carpet lay under my feet, muffling the squeaking noises often made by my trainers. Off the living room was a decently small kitchen space adjoined to a dining area which was raised higher.

My eyes swept across the beige and cream walls where portraits of sentimental value to Gerald and his fiancée hung, sometimes lounging, canoodling, or just staring awkwardly at each other. Good times, I thought. To me, the place looked as if nothing had been touched or moved from where it may have initially been. It was hard to tell because I had just walked in. How, then, had Gerald been mugged without showing some struggle?

I eyed the lounge area which was darker than the rest of the place because the light was glancing in the wide hallway which led there. There were poufy love seats that decked the checkered linoleum floor which stretched to the four open corners of the lounge; and yet another breezeway outside. It was funny how often I found myself somehow breaking and entering; was that how Roy had managed to enter my house?

Shrugging off that thought, I began strolling past the lounge and went to the breezeway.

A green yard punctuated with lovely scenery of pink and yellow daffodils and dandelions, withered willows and a picnic table set with a parasol and lounge seats lay to the left and right. A bubbly swimming pool which glistened under the sun also contributed to the great aesthetic view of the landscape.

Laden Hill is an upscale place where paramount, peripatetic and prosperous working classes live, fully furnished by apartments that could drain all my parents' savings for the entire year which belong to Larry Bernstein, the landlord. I would understand why Gerald would reside here; and why he had an Olympic-sized pool in his backyard.

Everything seemed all right *yet*. I needed to have a look at Gerald's work documents. I had a small still voice in my head telling me that maybe some clash at work with a colleague might have triggered his disappearance. Not so air-tight are the chances that that might be the answer to most disappearances, but it was a good point to start working from.

I found his study room upstairs hidden from the rest of the rooms just opposite a den. Den? That reminded me of Greens Association. Officer T had said that the boxes in his squad car had been confiscated as evidence behind whoever had kidnapped Gerald Kruger. But, I didn't proceed far with that thought so I began searching through the countless drawers and file cabinets in his small study area.

"Is work really this demanding?" I said to myself as I flipped over large folders which surprisingly were spotless.

Gerald kept most of his confidential documents in open places, so I had learned, and getting his resume, his personal documents, and even his coupons wasn't that strenuous. I rested myself on his cushy and plush leather seat and began leafing through the contents of a file he had scribbled PRIVATE on the top. Most of the papers here were unofficial, like his dentist appointment card, a birthday card, and other irrelevant things.

"Maybe it's not," I answered myself, shaking my head.

I spotted some patents he'd taken on his business products and the legal forms that prohibited his company, Tech World, to run under the management of Gerald. He looked like a very thorough man who loved his work, which made me think he must have haters. Yes! Every famous person today always encounters fans, critics, and haters; was this the case with Gerald going MFTL (Missing For Too Long)?

Seeing nothing of use, I returned all the files back into the drawers in no significant sequence and then went through some of his legal tenders. Obviously, besides the business greenhorns out there, everyone knows tenders really show the kind of partnership you have with which companies. I wasn't expecting this.

Standing out in a green cover was a tender made out to Greens Association among other bundles that were placed on a shelf. Great place to keep tenders Gerald, I chided silently, and opening the tender like it would reveal the answer to world peace.

There was an offer made by the MD of Greens Association, Mr. Greens to Gerald's Tech World for the shift of several interns to his company temporarily for one week. Gerald had signed to allow for the shift. Hmmm. Nothing so exciting, I realized. But then, I got another tingly wave all over my body. This innocent offer meant that the guys from Greens Association were definitely working for Gerald. Oops!

6

A Fiery Fate

The evening was slowly wrapping up, the sun reluctantly skimming the horizon with purple and red hues that looked oh-so-heavenly. Even more dazzling was when I saw the sunset through the frosty windscreen of my Parson as I steered my car into our garage. I realized Dad's car was already parked in, something I fought really hard to erase from my mind.

Had he found out that Roy Watson had 'broken in'? Or that I had broken in Gerald's apartment?

I backed the car in the driveway and prayed that it was just an awful dream. I walked in past the lobby off the kitchen, walking toward the arm chair in the lounge that Dad liked snoozing on. Just checking. It was summer, inarguably, but I wasn't expecting to find *both* Mom and Dad at home at this time. They looked surprised.

"Didn't we leave you *in-charge*?" Mom stood up and gave me a stare-down. If it wasn't for the anger that had darkened her features, she actually looked beautiful with her auburn hair, green slacks with a splash of red streaks and a loose white blouse. I forgot she had left to go to the consignment store in town. No wonder the odd fashion sense.

I gulped. "I wish I'd answer you, Mom. I took Jay out, and then we ended up in a load of trouble."

Dad stirred in his armchair, his blue eyes which struck a resemblance with mine glinting with concern. His graying brown hair and the permanent deep frown lines also gave him a fatherly look. "What trouble?"

"Is that some kind of twenty-first century lingo that your generation uses now?" he added, crossing his arms over his polo tee shirt.

I chuckled. "No Dad." The air constricted in my throat. I blew out in a slow and exhausted sigh. "Roy Watson was kidnapped," I muttered.

Mom planted her hands on the shiny gold belt that slithered around her tiny Cinderella waist. "What do you mean, Fred?" she asked, her tone flattening daftly.

"Roy Watson was kidnapped," I repeated. "A neighbor of his reported that he was seen being dragged away by an anonymous man." I didn't let on any farther than that. "Officer Timmons is working on that case. And so am *I*."

There was a period of silence, not long-lasting and bearable, that engulfed the lounge.

Dad spoke up. "That's...mysterious. Are you sure you're up to it to help find Roy Watson? As far as I can remember, he was that stuck-up kid who buried your head in a sandbox back in kindergarten."

"I...I...think." I let the words drag themselves.

Mom sank back in the seat and sighed. "Don't you think you're being too cynical? I know Roy. He put a snake in your jack-in-the-box toy once, and you had to get a tetanus shot for that." She rolled her eyes. "But, that doesn't give you the leeway to make up a silly story about him to save yourself from being grounded. That's low."

Now I was the one who slumped in a nearby seat, amazed. First, I didn't know Roy had almost *killed* me when we were young, and most important; Mom was thinking I was making it up was rather hurtful. No, very hurtful.

I began walking to my room upstairs. Suddenly, I wasn't really hungry. Mom and Dad had already proved they were not ready to believe me, so it was better if I went to relax a bit. All the excitement of the day had worn me out like a used rag. I wanted to just sink in my bed and drift to sleep. Then I remembered one disturbing thing: my nemesis needed my help. I needed to find him and Gerald before something nasty ensued. The burly man at the arcade, the gruesome shadow, and the creepy guy at the Hangout? Yeah, that scared the daylights and any lights out of me. But who was the guy, and what was his deal? The threat text? As my eyelids grew heavy, I already knew I was dealing with a mastermind.

Next morning, I was woken up to the weird shuffling sounds on my tiled floor which sounded like footfalls.

I shot up, grabbed my flashlight and cast the beam on the floor. The curtains were not drawn, and the predawn light wasn't doing me any help in lighting up my bedroom. Huddled over by my bed, looking haggard and sorrowful, were Dad and Mom. Oh no! First, they take my dignity away, now my privacy? Is being a teenager this paining?

I threw the blankets to the side and switched on the room lights. Mom walked to my side and began patting my back in a show of consoling me. Dad had brought a tray full of bagels, jelly doughnuts, and scones with tea and scrambled eggs and crusty bacon pieces.

"What's all this for?" I asked, ignoring that it was morning.

Mom gave Dad a slow nod and then set the tray across my lap. Dad looked at me with his blue eyes piercing the deepest part of my soul. "We're making up for what we said yesterday. And plus, you didn't eat supper yesterday. I know being a teenager is hard. Trust me, I know. But we trust you as our only child," he said tenderly, running his hand through my hair. "We acted like a bunch of unreasonable parents, *but* I think we were much better than most parents these days who..."

"Enough Luke," Mom stopped him with a place of a finger on his lips. "I think he got it. And I hope he has forgiven us and has accepted some cordial thanks from us?" she gave me a fascinating look.

"Of course!" I yelled excitedly, giving them bear hugs. *So much for the raise in allowance.* "The bagels are superb. And I like the powder sugar on the doughnuts. Nice."

"Thanks. My specialty." Mom edged on the bed, looking terrified. "But, Fred, is it true what you said. . .that Roy Watson was kidnapped?"

I nodded amid bites. "Yes, Mom; he and that renowned scientist who was in town. Gerald Kruger. Funny that they both were linked to one common thing: the science convention that was supposed to take place yesterday, but failed," I said. Seeing the confused stares from both of them, I added, "I know all this because...Officer Timmons filled me in. I am, of course, willing to find them." That part was truth.

Mom and Dad traded a knowing glance. "What would we expect from an amateur detective?" Dad joked, standing up. "Just make sure that you won't make this thing turn into a freak show. Because when a famous person is in trouble, as is Gerald Kruger, something shocking must always happen. Like the waterfall incident with Fred Guzzle."

I gnawed on my trembling lip. Was he joking now, or was it the Daddy-gone-serious guy talking? Then an idea sprang to my mind. "Um, Mom and Dad, did you both get a weird phone call, blank text or video/photo sent to your phones yesterday?"

Mom shrugged. "No."

Dad followed suit, frowning. "Why?"

I smiled. "It's nothing. Have a nice day." Watching their retreating figures, the small still voice in the back of my head suddenly grew very loud. *Just the lead you needed.*

While it was teeming with people in the streets, others were driving in cars, and the sun beating angrily on the heads of those who weren't lucky enough to have visors and pith helmets, the inside of GPD HQ's was contrastingly chilly, damp and musty. Some combination you would only find in a morgue! Parking my car outside, I hoped for any good news available.

I ran smack-dab into Officer Timmons who was conversing almost silently with his secretary, Jermaine Todd in the lobby. His frizzy brown hair was now freed from the bondage of a police cap, flowing to his ears and I could see from the deep lines around his brown eyes that he was under stress. The last time I'd seen him, he was totally worked up with finding Gerald and Roy. Had he found anything useful?

"Don't set your hopes too high, Fred," he chided as he walked me to his office. "Twenty-four hours and *we* haven't turned up anything, and you think you have a clue? That's so cute, but I'm not buying it."

Whoa! Had the sleep deprivation also taken away his cheerful mood and optimism with it?

"It's not far-fetched, but I think it will help pretty well; Officer T," I told him. Telling him about the man at the arcade and the Hangout made me tremble even after thinking about it severally. "I think I might have run into him yesterday at the arcade, but I tried telling you only to realize Roy was gone."

"You think he might be behind all this?" Officer Timmons asked, settling in his officer seat and leaning on his desk.

I fished out the tenders I got from Gerald's apartment and passed them to him. Casually, I said, "I got those from a friend who works for Greens Association. He's a keeper. They indicate that Mr. Green sent some guys from his company down to TechWorld to work for Gerald as interns temporarily for a week."

As I might have expected from a strong man like Officer T, he slammed his fist right on his desk, toppling some pens on the carpeted floor. I sat rigidly on my seat, not because it was cheaply made from solid mahogany, but because I knew where Officer T was headed.

"Do you know what that means Fred?" he asked with a less-than-frivolous tone.

Um...that I was a genius for having found the tender?

"That we only have one week to find where a renowned scientist and his nutty PR agent has disappeared to!

Do you know how hard that can be?" His voice was shaking with anger. "I can't believe I'm working on a case about a guy whose show I didn't even get invited to," he lamented.

"Me too," I added grimly. "Anyway, I think the guy I was talking about might be working for GA. Maybe he's part of a large scam, what do you think?"

Officer Timmons swiveled his chair and faced the large French window beside his shelves of silverware which overlooked Laden Hill, that top-class residential area, the distant Glades River and the shining sun over it. He had to be thinking or else how would I have explained the way he was mumbling and staring at the tender?

"Officer, I assume we should work with what we have at the moment. There's no reason to rush in, but we have to start with something," I added, sighing at the bleakness of my words. What was I saying? Gerald and Roy were running out of time – that was a reason to *rush*, wasn't it?

There was a click at the door, and a lady with tanned blue slacks, a clingy white blouse, and clunky stiletto shoes slipped in, her cheeks reddening as her eyes swept from me to Officer Timmons and back. A look of contempt flashed across her green eyes as she gave me a discreet once-over; and then sat at the seat across me. I had nothing against her, but her suspicious character wasn't all pleasing to me. I held my breath.

"Oh, hello, Dina. I was hoping you'd have been here earlier, but it's forgivable that you're two minutes late," Officer Timmons said, recovering from his somber state and leaping to his feet to shake the lady's hand. It was bony, frosty, and had a lot of marks around the wrist and knuckles.

"It's so chivalrous of you not to hold it against me," Dina purred, fondling Officer T's hand for too long that I thought she had glued hers on his.

I felt uncomfortable at once and stood from my seat, excused myself, and walked out of the office. Was it suddenly chilly outside than inside? I guess talking about Gerald and Roy had really taken some of the heat off me. I decided to go and order a nice cold Cola at the refreshments bar which was not far from the GPD building. Surprisingly, it became like a thousand degrees outside as I strode to the nearest ice-cream parlor which was just opposite Marcy's Flower Shop.

The one-mile walk had already drained me out of the energy that I had accumulated after eating my delicious breakfast. I walked in the refreshments store which was owned by a great friend of mine, Gregg Mullin and ordered a Cola, a banana split, and scrumptious-looking summer treats that he was offering.

Again, I couldn't resist asking Gregg whether he'd gotten any anonymous phone call or blank text.

Just the reaction I had waited for; an emphatic shake of the head. As I walked out fifteen minutes later, I snuck a look at my watch. Ten thirty was the perfect time for me to drop by Jay's and Jolene's homes and update them. My walk went uninterrupted, except for the chit-chatting from the people, noises from the kids who were fighting over a candy bar at the park, and...

BOOM!

All those noises suddenly didn't make sense to me as I rushed down Wilson Street with sweat streaming down my back and my sneakers squeaking loudly as they pounded against the sidewalk. I was shocked when my eyes landed on the smoke spewing out of the entrance to the Glades Police Department HQ! Minutes later, a raging fire would start!

7

Help from the Dark

Like lightning, I frantically called 911 on my phone, careful to tell the lady on the other end of the line how disastrous the smoke seemed and how horrendous it would render the GPD building on Wilson Street if it went uncontrolled for not so long.

Finally, my legs stopped quivering and I stood beside my Parson staring at the thick foggy smoke that blanketed the entire front of the building. Concerned bystanders had been drawn to the scene like bees to honey, looking apprehensive about the smoke. Others just shook their heads in disapproval; while other obnoxious people began pinching their noses and faked hacking coughs.

Immediately, I called Jay and Jolene; and told them to meet me just outside the GPD building. The sickening feeling that maybe Officer Timmons and other personnel were still inside, perhaps dying or already engulfed by the noxious fumes, made the inside of my stomach knot.

As everyone stood outside, their faces crestfallen, a body dragged itself helplessly through the front door of the building, gasping for breath and slumped on the pavement in a heap.

"Who's that?" someone asked, pointing fearfully.

"Obviously, a survivor," another replied with a snort. I turned my eyes towards the respondent and saw a wiry man with curly black hair, rimless glasses, and sporting a pressed navy blue suit. His hair was tucked under a formal-looking cap which had a blazon: Glades Glamour. He *had* to be a reporter.

And I have never liked reporters; especially those with a big ego, bad dress codes, and a bigger mouth that's twice the ego. No pun intended.

Before I could talk him up, flashing lights and blaring sirens became the order of the next hour. Firefighters donning red dungarees, masks over their mouths, and heat-resistant gloves rushed out of a red truck gripping hosepipes or fire extinguishers and into the building.

I snuck a look at the reporter and grimaced. Instead of being full of empathy, he was actually talking to a camera being held by his assistant!

Over at the terrace, I saw a haggard-looking and tired Jasmine Todd coltishly walking out of the building, held upright by two brawny firefighters. She came near me, held my ear to her mouth, and whispered in a wilting voice, "Save Officer Timmons for me. Please do."

I could not help but nod hesitantly, sneaking a glance again at the Reporter Guy who shot a curt nod at my way, and shrugged.

The more I thought about that guy, the more I began feeling angered and aggravated. Back to the scenario; the smoke had ebbed away, leaving behind formless charred debris and a faint smell of...

"Is that lithium I smell?" Jolene asked as soon as she parked her RLX-Super behind my car and bounded out hastily in a daze. Jay was trailing behind her, bewildered.

"Maybe," I told her. "Nothing's been reported yet. It would be funny to a complete fool if I said that because the police aren't here to investigate. Just look at how drab the building looks now."

Jay nodded drearily and then turned to Jolene. "Why do you think about lithium?" he asked.

"Because it's mostly used in batteries; and when batteries explode, the reactive lithium could cause such an effect and burn through almost any material," Jolene explained. "Probably something operating on lithium batteries must have overheated and blown up."

"Or some*one*," I added darkly.

Suddenly, I found a huge fuzzy microphone shoved under my nose and a camera directed at my surprised face. Standing beside me with the most counterfeit smile on his sparkling exfoliated face, (I suppose), and his arm coiled around my shoulders; was the nagging wino reporter.

"What's...happening?" I stuttered, pushing aside the microphone and wiping off the accumulative dust from the mic.

"The whole USA is ready to hear your opinions about the tragic fire accident that just took place here at the Glades Police Department," he drawled in a Canadian accent. "My name's Dart Preston, working as an unpaid but patient field reporter for GG. And you, esteemed interviewee, are?"

Jay grabbed the mouthpiece from his collar and chucked it towards the road. Dart's voice was now inaudible through the camera. "We are fed up with interviews and are ready to *leave*! So, if you don't mind, I'm in need of some time away from nagging reporters," Jay fumed, frowning angrily at Dart Preston.

Dart smiled at the camera and dug into his pocket shirt, removed a slick gizmo with a mini screen and an inbuilt speaker, and clipped it on his collar. "Lucky for me, I have a digital electronic voice amplifier which surprisingly looks one-fiftieth its original size; but still costs forty dollars." He flipped his curly hair away from his hazel eyes which harbored complacence. "Young money."

I rolled my eyes at Dart Preston. "No comment," I said simply.

"Sure, you don't wanna comment 'cause I just heard you say someone must have been behind this fire,"

Dart Preston, the curly-haired college freak, contradicted. "Does that mean it was sabotage?"

"No comment kindly," Jolene pleaded, elbowing Dart to the side and planting her palm on the camera screen. "That's if you really don't want me to turn things ugly."

Dart persisted. Typical of reporters in Glades. "Well, are you all some sort of detectives? Because no one is frequently unwilling to answer, 'nagging reporters' as much as detectives, spies, circus clowns, or talking dogs;" he said, sniggering at his lame joke briefly before adding, "and you, my friends, look like detectives."

I turned a skeptical look at Jay and Jolene who were shaking their heads sadly. Was this guy really thinking we were dumb enough to break our cover in front of the entire country? No way, bro.

"*Get lost,*" Jay whispered, clenching his teeth and cracking his knuckles.

Dart Preston gulped, backed away, and gave a shrug of annoyance as he pranced off alongside his assistant.

As soon as we were able to evade Dart Preston and his cameraman, we realized the smoke was now history, and officers were lingering in and about the charred and crispy building, probably looking for clues.

"Let's check in with Dylan Peterson about the lithium theory," I suggested, walking up to the head firefighter who was conversing with a couple of his buddies morosely.

"Hi, guys. Nasty fire, huh?" Dylan remarked, his eyes combing the charred building.

We all nodded despondently. "Do you have any leads?" I asked.

His eyes went back to his iPod, and he began scrolling down a few of his typed notes. "Well, there is a fatal amount of already-detonated lithium-based minute frags that have been found in Officer Timmons' office and the verandah close to it." He paused and gave us a look of sheer fright. "That means someone was after that old yet fine-tuned machine of a man."

We didn't need clarification to know that was frightening. I gasped. "He hasn't been removed from the building since the fire. Is he…okay?" I asked.

Dylan bit his lip and shook his head. "No sign of an unidentified body or his body as well, but I'll brief you when something comes our way," he said, shook our hands and got lost in the crowd of firefighters.

We walked to my car feeling depressed by the outcome. Me, I felt overwhelmed by whatever had taken place in the last few days. Despite my being an amateur detective, I couldn't find my way out of this maze of confusion.

"At least I was right about lithium," Jolene said, sighing happily.

"What next, Fred?" Jay asked, kicking a pebble off the sidewalk.

I scratched my chin. "Let's go through all this one more time, just to ensure we have our priorities on the right side," I offered. "Gerald Kruger goes missing, his PR agent follows, then the GPD goes up in flames, and Officer T is nowhere to be found."

"Sad," Jolene commented. "What about suspects?" she asked.

"Hmmm, we do have that fussy Dart Preston. I don't know what he may be guilty of, but he's all I got," I said. Indeed, we were hopeless. But I wasn't going to pigeonhole that guy at the arcade on Saturday. "What's the name of that guide whom we found at the arcade on Monday, Jay?" I asked, knowing that Jay was not good with names.

As Jay shrugged, Jolene's brows shot up. "Gosh! Why didn't I think of that guy? He's McHale's elder brother, Jimmy McHale. He was the head guide and showed us a lot of stuff around the arcade," she said in a monotoned voice. "What about him?"

I rolled my eyes. "*He* is our next suspect. I caught him the other day at the Hangout with a familiar girl. I think she's the library assistant," I said, deep in thought. "She's the same lady whom I met with Officer T not so long ago today.
Anything weird about that?"

A moment passed then the three of us all leaped in surprise almost simultaneously. "She set this whole thing up! *She* is our other suspect!" Jay shrieked, calling too much attention to himself.

Apparently, too much attention.

At the corner of the block, a shadowy figure with a dark poncho, glinting visors, and a cap peaked and then quickly drew back. Jimmy McHale? I wasn't affirmative about it, even though he had been spooking me frequently like that.

"Who was that?" Jolene asked, sounding terrified.

"No idea," I whispered back. Moving from the terrace, I signaled them to follow me. "I think we're about to find out."

"I'm tired of surprises. Let's go get us a stalker!" Jay said, smiling.

Bracing our backs against the wall, we slowly made our way past a cordon of cops (they'd be useful if we got nabbed) and back to the alleyway at the side of the building. Poor lighting and the dreadful number of trashcans which fostered stray cats made it difficult for us to make out the set of eyes that only stood out amidst the dense darkness.

"Who are you?" Jay hollered bravely, his voice trembling slightly out of uncertainty.

The stalker slowly emerged from the gloom, pulled back his poncho, and smiled cheekily.

A smile like that could only belong to him and him alone. "It's me, Danson McHale," he said, glancing nervously at Jolene and uneasily at Jay and me. . "And I bet I can help you guys out."

8
Back to Square One

What?" Jay, Jolene, and I gasped in surprise.

It seemed so unlikely that Danson, the younger brother of our prime suspect was offering to help us in the case. Normally I'd take it that he was nuts, but as a detective, I didn't want to overlook any possibility.

"Don't act all surprised," Danson said, removing the cap and his poncho. He nodded at Jolene. "I told you all about my brother, Jimmy. Don't you remember?"

Jolene gulped and shook her head ruefully. "I guess I might have zoned out," she said dully.

"Huh?" Danson asked.

"Jo!" I chided playfully, giving Danson a wry smile. "She may have forgotten, that's all. Anyway, I don't think we've met officially." I extended my hand and shook his sweaty palm. "I'm Fred Turner. You have met my two best friends, Jay and Jolene."

Danson nodded courteously, revealing his set of pearl-white teeth and laugh lines below his freckled forehead. He did bear a resemblance with Jimmy McHale. "Thank you so much. By the way, I have heard of your name before," he said, stopping to stare hard at the sky.

What did he mean by that? Last time I checked, I wasn't very famous in Glades. It's a sleepy small town that's why.

"Oh! From my bro, Jimmy and his friends, that's where," he said, nodding his head.

Jay and Jolene gave me vacant looks. How could our prime suspect know me? As much as that sounded unusual, I couldn't help but feel a chill course down my spine.

"How?" I asked, giving Danson a look of doubt under furrowed brows. How else was I supposed to react to such news? Apparently, I happen to be very splendid with my emotions. I can hide some, but some I find it hard to put under control.

Danson pointed towards the city center with his cap. "Why don't we go to Jimmy's house and I'll show you how," he offered. I couldn't see the look in his eyes under the glasses, but he seemed convincingly *convincing*. But there was this feeling below my skin which didn't agree. One thing about me; I trust my instincts. They are totally infallible.

Jay rubbed his hands together and smiled at Danson. "If that means we get to wrap this case up…"

"Are you detectives?" Danson cut in, his eyebrows elevating. I steadied Jay and Jolene with a glance and turned to Danson.

"Maybe, but if you're willing to cooperate we could work together to find out who kidnapped Gerald Kruger," I suggested, giving him a sincere look. "He just might thank us by giving us all free invites to his convention!"

"Sweet!" Danson whooped.

Jay, still looking confused, asked, "So whose hot wheels are we burning today?"

I glanced wearily at my Parson over at the curb. It couldn't hold a candle to Jolene's RLX, I thought.

"Let's take my car," Jolene offered, jiggling her car keys. As Danson headed for the passenger seat, she whispered to me, "Ride. I can't even believe you let this guy work with us. He's a wacko!"

"It's better if we send a wacko to catch another wacko," I said to her, winking.

Jolene sighed. "Whatever. Let's just go."

I climbed into the driver's seat, took a last look at my car, and then inserted the key into the ignition. Jolene's RLX is not just the in-thing now, but its state-of-the-art and very smooth to handle. Unlike my two-year-old car, her RLX had an automatic braking system, strong shock absorbers, hi-tech graphical view of each and every part of the engine, electricity panels to check the flow of currents on which it operates, and the wildest stereo system in the twenty-first century. Wow! That puts a damper on my car, doesn't it?

As I pulled away, my mind was whirring from all the jumbled-up ideas floating in it. How were Gerald and Roy fairing on? Was Jimmy really behind their kidnapping? Was Danson leading us to a trap? That was the scariest part because he really looked intent. By trying to extrapolate what was bound to happen from what had already taken place, I only felt I was worsening the situation. I had been threatened – who knew what my presence in Jimmy's place would lead me to?

"He lives on Triton Street, next to Laden Hill where Gerald Kruger lives with his fiancée, Heather," Jolene informed me as she researched for her mini-laptop. She's the whizz-kid among us, and she always tries not to rub it in our faces. "It's quite a populated area and most of the population resides in shacks or dilapidated detached houses."

"True," Danson conceded, looking surprised. "Guys, I really need to tell you one thing; my brother is not entirely guilty. You may be wondering why I just spontaneously joined forces with you." He paused, his face taking on a look of worry. "I don't know what has been going on with Jimmy these days. I mean, since he got fired from a fancy internship job last month, he's been acting up lately."

"How?" I asked, driving along the bustling city center.

Danson shrugged. "He had an internship job with some company in town. I can't quite place the name, though.

He had it going on smoothly until he mysteriously got sacked. It has really affected him," he said.

"Then how did he get the job as a guide?" Jay asked.

"Well, *that* is what I think he might be guilty of," Danson agreed. "I don't even know how he landed that one-time occupation, but I do know he could have gotten in through the back door."

"Back doors have never been good," Jay said sarcastically. "You bump your little toe against them, crash into people through them, and even lock yourself out when the key gets lost."

"Huh?" Danson asked.

"Never mind. Let's get a brunch first," I said, slowing down the car near a famous restaurant. The backstreet wasn't very busy, so there was ample parking space. Before I could pull up, Danson grabbed my arm and pointed at the entrance to the restaurant. "Who's that?"

"That's one of Jimmy's buddies," Danson hissed. "That means Jimmy might be around here somewhere."

Jolene scoffed, "So what, Danny?"

"Oh, you finally got me a nickname," Danson cooed at Jolene.

"Drop the act, numbskull," Jolene shot back, clearly florid with anger.

Danson leaned forward and peered at the guy standing outside the restaurant.

"He's big trouble, Fred. I know he's quite the gambler so maybe that's why he's here," he clarified.

I monitored the guy's movements: from a rigid standing posture, then a slouchy bending poise as if he was picking something from the ground, back to his erect posture, and then began striding quickly to a slick Mercedes parked nearby. That was some act! Was our man getting away?

"What did he just do?" Jay asked, squinting under the bright sunlight.

I bit my lip, looking back at where he had been standing. "Over at the sidewalk, next to the guardrail where a couple of benches have been placed," I said with a feeling of fright.

"I can't see anything," Jolene complained.

My eyes could have been deceiving me, but was that blinking thingamajig he'd placed on the ground? It could have been, but I wasn't sure. I remembered the threat I had been sent yesterday. Was this the way the culprit was trying to make me regret having not been invited? By trying to nearly kill or kidnap everyone I knew? Who was he/she trying to kill or kidnap now?

Danson finally jumped out of the car and raced to where the guy had been standing. He bent over, touched the seemingly innocuous red thingy, and waved us to come.

"He *is* daring," I admitted, locking the car as the three of us rushed to his side. A closer look at the LED light on the flashing chip made me realize that we were in grave trouble. "Is it an incendiary chip, you know like those which blow up…uh-oh."

Just as the words came out of my mouth, so fast and frighteningly, the same guy who had placed the chip dashed towards us, dressed in a long dark overcoat and dark race-driver glasses, and grabbed Danson by his waist. Jolene accidentally tumbled and fell as the man lugged Danson to the car.

Two heavy-set masked men appeared out of the hotel, and then with a look of sudden astonishment, they lunged at Jay and me and began wrestling us. It was crazy that it was deserted; and even calling for help would have been the last thing on our minds as they pulled us away from the sidewalk.

"Who are you guys?" I asked, trying to wriggle out of the man's iron biceps.

Of course, they didn't answer. They were busy stalling us as the other man pushed Danson into the back seat of his car. It all happened so fast; the men pinned us down, managed to silence Jolene from her whining and then like Bolt, scrambled inside the Mercedes and drove away.

My head was banging loudly, and my arms were aching from the struggle.

We looked sadly as the car peeled away into the unknown, Danson's pale face staring back at us with a nebulous look.

"There goes our only lead," I announced, feeling the weight of my words fall on my shoulders. "What next?"

9

Conspiracies

An hour later, we were seated in my room, Jolene with her laptop in t the recliner, Jay fiddling with the chip by my bed, and I was lying on my bed staring at the ceiling; wishing I had never gotten involved with such a case. Twenty-one hours after Gerald had gone missing and we didn't have any major breakthrough. If you want to know how depressing that is, then fit in my shoes and feel the grief.

It was not too long before his disappearance started to raise a national alarm and set the media abuzz. And Dart Preston as well. Now, it was just as if we hadn't been doing anything. I had tried calling other police stations, but there was still no sign of Danson and his kidnapper.

"Hmm, it seems this chip was set as a trap so that Danson could be snatched away," Jay reasoned, gnawing on the chip curiously and then making a disgusted look. "Yuck, it even tastes horrible. Jo, what do you think?"

"Well, nanotechnology is really taking the center stage at these times so we might as well deduce that our man is a genius," Jolene said, typing on the keypad. "We're dealing with a *nerd*."

I rose from my bed and supported myself against the window. "Do you think we might be treading on dangerous grounds?" I asked ominously.

Jay chuckled good-naturedly. "I live for danger, Fred. And you know that," he said. "What's on your mind?"

I turned to Jolene and said, "Can you look up Greens Association's payroll list and the internship program? I have a feeling our man may have a connection." Smiling back at Jay, I added, "Remember the cartons that Officer T found in Gerald's apartment; and how the mystery man said Gerald's disappearance was for the good of GA? That pretty much tells me our man undoubtedly has to have a link with GA."

"I like how you reason, Fred. But do you know that GA is still the place we applied for our internship, and that means that we could have brushed shoulders very easily with our mystery dude?" Jay said, his eyes staring absent-mindedly at the chip.

"That's it!" I paused to let all that info seep through my brain. "But that still doesn't answer the main question here: Why did he kidnap Gerald Kruger – and Roy?"

Jolene cleared her throat slightly and said, "Come take a look at this. Interesting information, I must say." Jay and I huddled around the screen with anticipation. "I've accessed the records for GA which didn't turn up anything suspicious apart from the job applications of you two and a bunch of other high school kids." She turned to Jay with a smirk. "A janitor's faggot? *Real* mature."

"Hey! Nothing's ever been better," Jay said defensively.

"Can you find the job applications for last month?" I asked Jolene. "If Jimmy had been working legally in GA, then they ought to have kept his records, isn't it?"

"Guess so. That'll also prove that Danson was telling the truth and he's not a big jerk as he sounds," Jolene added with a not-so-funny tone.

A long list appeared on-screen with names of people who had applied for the May internship. I ran my finger along the column, but Jimmy's name wasn't there.

"Bingo," Jay said. "So, Danson was telling the truth after all."

I decided to fill them in on the tenders I had found in Gerald's apartment which showed that Mr. Green had shifted some of his workers to Tech World for a temporal internship program; until the convention was over.

"Hmmm," Jolene muttered thoughtfully. "That means somebody in the shift list must be behind the disappearances. This case sure has a lot of drama."

"Yup, and as soon as we're done, I'm going to the beach," Jay added as he flipped over on the couch.

"I think we need a plan. As we all know, we have four of our key leads missing, two suspects under the radar, and only three of us to solve this case before it leaks to the media;" I said, thinking about Dart Preston. Sure, hope he'd shut that mouth of his *if* he found out, I told myself.

"We could split up," Jay suggested.

"I will look up the list of interns and send a copy of it to your computer, Fred," Jolene said, shutting down her laptop and placing it beside my PC. "Then maybe I'll drop by Roy's home and tell his parents not to worry about his absence."

"I'll stick with you, Fred. Two's company," Jay said, rolling his eyes at Jolene. Those two never agree unless I intervene.

"Let's go look up Jimmy's place and see if we can find anything," I said, clapping my hands in triumph. "Great! We got a plan. That weird lady who almost blew up GPD and nabbed Officer T is on the cops wanted list, but it wouldn't hurt keeping an eye on her."

"Okay," Jolene said.

"Deal," Jay agreed.

Just then, we heard a soft rap on the door, and Mom stuck in her head. She had a look of doubt, surprise, and apprehension all evenly distributed on her browned face.

"What are you guys up to?" she asked inquisitively.

"Um…devising a way to find Roy Watson," I spoke up. "We're worried if he doesn't show up, we'll have to call his parents and tell them their son's lost."

Mum wrinkled her nose. "Well then, it's good to see that you kids are doing something great for the kid who almost got you three expelled from kindergarten by planting video game cartridges in your backpacks," she said, snorting.

"Wow!" Jay exclaimed, scratching his ruffled hair. "The more I think about it, the more I fear we're actually repaying evil with good. And to think I loved video games; and they almost got me kicked out of kindergarten."

Mum giggled. "Anyway, lunch is ready. I'm serving sautéed potatoes with lamb chops and a salad," she declared, slipping away and lumbering downstairs.

Jolene and Jay turned skeptical glances at me. I hated it when they thought my mother was eccentric.

Well, Triton Street is not exactly as Jolene had described it earlier, but it sure did look cramped and in a bad state. The shacks always lean on to each other, making the pathways between them constrict and the place to look like a slum. Especially in summer, Triton Street dwellers usually lounge or even camp near the moor just west of Glades Natural Forest because that's when everything goes to a standstill; from the water supply; to power, and even food.

"Maybe Jimmy is not a huge earner," Jay commented as we drove across the dirt road meandering through the moor. "Anyone living in such a state would be, don't you think?"

I nodded, letting my gaze to wander off the road and to the shacks that dotted the landscape to my right. Apart from the scattered trees which offered relief to the dwellers, there was no greenery past the moor. No wonder they all camped there, for the sake of survival.

"I think you're right. Looking back at what Danson said, that may have been the reason he illegally got the job as a guide at the convention," I said.

We rode on silently until the dirt road paved the way for a dusty pathway which eventually disappeared right at the brink of an old house with weak frames, broken windows, and scraped out stucco. Even without assuming, I knew this had to be the case with almost all the houses here.

I pulled in, and we got out, ignoring the murky water and mushy soil that squished under our shoes. The last thing on the minds of the people living here was to think we were disgracing them by putting on a show of pride.

"Where is Jimmy's house?" Jay asked, his eyes scanning the crowded place.

I shrugged and nodded to some locals sitting beside a hammock, busy chattering silently.

An old man on the hammock was nursing his swollen leg and reclining it on a rock. I could see the pain in his eyes as we got closer. His friends turned their heads to us almost in unison and blinked in contempt.

Jay nudged my arm and narrowed his eyes. He was probably telling me to make a move.

"Um...hey there. I'm Fred Turner, and this is my friend Jay Clarke," I called out, swallowing a gulp of nervousness. These men looked rather aggressive for their age. Like an older version of gangbusters.

The old man on the hammock broke into a spasm of painfully booming coughs and then sighed vehemently. *Oh my God, we made him do that, didn't we?* He gave us a cold look through his watery eyes. Whatever was irking this guy remained a mystery to me even as we proceeded to talk with the other group of old people.

"Do you know where Jimmy McHale's house is?" I asked politely to the other men.

A man with silvery hair and a bald spot clenched his cane and directed it to a house which looked pretty much as run-down as the others.

"Thanks for that," Jay said, rolling his eyes furtively. He turned to me. "Don't these guys ever talk? And what's up with that old man at the hammock? He didn't look like the welcoming type; more like the throw-a-stone-at-your-face type."

"I don't know about him," I said as we excused ourselves from the group.

Clearly, with all the tension about the disappearances, it made it easier if we didn't make any more enemies.

"Maybe it's the gout," Jay remarked, giggling. He met the stern look in my eyes and stopped. "Sorry. I'm critically sarcastic."

"Well, now don't be. This case is getting pretty intense, and if we don't find Gerald Kruger anytime sooner, it's going to go viral," I said, walking up to the front door; or what had remained of it. I reached for the knob and then retracted my hand as I felt a fine powder on my palm. I couldn't resist from taking a whiff. "Um...is this...gun powder?" I asked, feeling more horrified than surprised.

Jay ran his finger on my palm and smelt the substance. "You bet, Fred. What would gun powder be doing on the doorknob of a house?" he asked, petrified. Then his eyes zoned in on the door mat at the stoop. "It looks unevenly laid. Maybe..."

He bent and pulled the mat away. A bullet-like object dropped on the floorboard and rolled away. "This is epic!" He gushed; and then added, "I mean, disturbing. Do you think this is a trap?" I couldn't answer him then because of the tension build-up in my mind. The mastermind was playing mind games with us. I stood to my normal height and then gasped as I saw a figure hovering inside Jimmy's house, with the trademark cloak and sunglasses on. I pulled Jay to the side of the window and pointed at the person inside.

"Maybe it's Jimmy," Jay whispered.

"With a cloak and sunglasses? I beg to differ, Mon frère," I said, squinting inside the room. It looked like the WWE had a brawl in there; scattered clothes, cluttered dishes, and even book piles all over. "Somebody really needs to do a clean-up."

We watched as the man in the cloak restlessly paced in the room, kicking stuff and then plopping on the only seat in the room. Oh, I mean, the only seat in the room *without* clutter. The guy seemed to be impatient but he really knew how to smother his emotions under the cloak and cape.

"We're just wasting our time here, Fred. Tomorrow's work day and we're here trailing somebody who was about to kill us just minutes ago with a mini-bomb!" Jay whined, burying his head in his palms.

I cupped his mouth and shoved his head down as the man began walking towards the window. Terror filled Jay's eyes as the man's arm swooped down near his head and pulled it back. I was guessing he was leaning against the window as his elbow emerged at the edge of the wooden sill and I heard him sigh. That was close! However, his elbow was two inches away from my nose. Any slight movement would destroy our plan to sneak in Jimmy's house; 0that is if it was his house in the first place.

I heard a click and then the man's raspy voice talking through the phone.

I was glad it was on loudspeaker because the receiver's voice was very audible through the speaker.

"Jimmy, where are you? I've been waiting here for one hour," the man grunted, evidently livid. "You better have a solid explanation, or else our collaboration will wither."

"I know that, Spencer. Here's the deal, I've got the money and the air tickets. The only good thing about that is I will now stop risking my precious life again."

The man made a gurgling sound through his throat. "What do you mean?" he asked.

"I'll make it clearer this time. I am having *my* share of the profit, and you are not going to get any part of it," Jimmy said, chuckling evilly. "I'm headed to our now-not-secret hideout to bring an end to all this."

I gave Jay a triumphant smile. This only meant that we were very close to finding the real answers.

"Are you quitting?" Spencer chortled, "Because you and I know surrender was not part of the terms and conditions of our deal."

Jimmy chuckled again. "I am, but with the total share of the money, having taken my revenge and fulfilled *my* part of the deal," he said. "Well, that'll only be after I dispose those three meddling kids and our hostages."

Hostages!

Jay rolled his eyes and mimicked a knife slicing his throat. I gulped at the dimness of the revelation.

Jimmy and Spencer had been behind all this…but would it come to an end?

Spencer shut his phone in an outburst of anger and banged the sill in anger. My heart leaped in shock as Spencer began walking to the front door. Oops! I grabbed Jay's arm and we took a leap over the wooden rails and into the concealment of tall flowers and dense bushes flanking the side of the house.

Spencer walked out, took a few tentative steps outside and in a split second a deafening blast sounded, and I felt a heat-wave blowing across my face. If I was right, which I thought I was, Spencer had literally taken the blow that had been set up for *us*.

"This is our chance. To the rear," I said to Jay as people began running towards the house.

Jay looked at me with a surprised look and shook his head ruefully as we ran to the back entrance. "Fred, this is the worst day ever!"

10
Dead End

You think he's gonna be all right?" Jay asked nervously as soon as we reached the back of the house. "I mean, you saw how he almost blew up in smithereens. That was scary, not epic as such, but really scary."

I caught my breath as we made a stop and said, "So far, that's one of the weirdest things I've seen happening since we started this case." I looked over at the pile of tin cans that were lodged between the backdoor and the neighboring house's picket fence. "I think this is the weirdest thing ever. The back door's obviously inaccessible and now that there are people at the front, we have no choice."

Jay nodded glumly then pointed at an open hatch at the top of the door. "*But* we do have a plan B," he said, twitching his eyebrows up and down. "I could give you a leg-up and then stay here and be on the lookout. It can't be that hard."

I patted Jay's shoulder gratefully. "Thanks a lot. At least this time I won't have to go through the dreaded backdoors," I joked.

"You sure won't," Jay said, smiling.

He hoisted me up on his shoulders, and I reached for the hatch, my fingers clutching at the edges. I pulled myself in, wriggling my upper body and then withdrawing my legs. I gave Jay a thumbs-up and plummeted in the dark room; it still looked like a mess although there were a few clean spots on what seemed to be a counter and a shelf.

I was in the store room. From inside, I could see Jay keeping vigil; which meant that whoever was in could see whoever was outside, but not vice versa. Contented, I began feeling my way through the small space. I'm not claustrophobic, but I was beginning to hyperventilate as I thought how painful it'd be if the walls began to close in.

The odds of me succeeding in my snooping without some light to help me go about were a gazillion to one in this creepy store. I dug in my pockets, fished out my tiny flashlight and shone the beam across the fraction of the floor which wasn't covered with grimy overalls or cans of paint or hammers.

I pushed open the door, and it made a creaking sound which reverberated down the hallway that was to the left. *Good one, Fred.* I cast the beam down the empty hallway and followed it until I reached the landing of a spiral staircase which led to the lounge. That had been where I had spotted Spencer. I could still hear some people chit-chatting outside – and a police car!

Shrugging those thoughts, I followed the hallway and descended a tiny flight of stairs to another room. This one had the lock on, and unfortunately, it needed a card to open it. Terrific! How in the world…?

A bulb went on in my mind as I fumbled for the pass card in my pocket. Since I began thinking that the pass card was somehow mysterious, I always walked with it just in case I needed it. And after a day, it had come to be of great use to me. At the moment, I didn't even care how Roy knew it could open doors; I was too excited.

A series of commands ran down a small screen on the lock, and then a low computer voice said: 'Thumbprint Required.'

Thumbprint! Whose? Mine, Roy's, Gerald's, or anyones…

My ears pricked suddenly as I felt some movement just near me. Flicking the flashlight to my side, I ran it along the passage to what looked like an underground entrance. How did I get from the store room to the underground? There had to be some explaining for Jimmy to do. That's if he hadn't flown with the money to God-knows-where.

I ignored the metal clanging sound and went on with the lock system, figuring out that maybe it wanted *my* thumbprint. Wasn't that the reason Roy had given me? In all the tension and suspense, I placed my right thumb on the glowing blue pad and held my breath.

One second later, a bing sound rang, and the voice replied: 'Access Granted.'

I couldn't describe the whooshing feeling I felt in my gut the minute that door slid open by the sides, and a fog machine blinded my eyes with purple and blue fog. I felt as if I had just walked in the wrong place. Immediately I stepped in, the floor began glowing with patterns of red neon, and the walls adopted a hue of many colors.

"Where am I?" I whispered, my eyes roaming around the room. The fog hadn't settled, but I could see the computer panels, the surveillance camera panel and the cool equipment hanging in display cases.

My mind went back to the equipment belonging to Greens Association that had been destroyed and found in Gerald's apartment. I wasn't sure, but maybe they could have come from here. Frankly, I had many questions flowing in my mind right now. It sounded amusing that there had been a nasty scenario just outside this house, and no one was even daring to come and investigate inside. I guess there is a need for detectives like me.

Taken aback by the technological stuff I was feasting with my eyes, I decided to take a look at the surveillance cameras. Two out of the six screens on the panel had broken down, but the remaining showed the view as in was at the backyard, the lounge, the outside porch, and…the arcade!

Whoever owned this place really knew how to follow someone. The arcade looked deserted due to the convention being canceled and how the public suddenly became uninterested.

That was what the culprit had wanted, I thought.

There were a few police officers searching around the living room, moving couches, and turning over tables and chairs. I looked keenly and saw Dylan on the porch, some meds carrying a stretcher with a body, Spencer's, and some analysts at the door with Dylan. I just hoped the bomb hadn't been lethal enough to kill Spencer. We needed him as a suspect.

But that wasn't the only thing I was hoping: since everyone in the footage seemed to be oblivious of the cameras, I hoped the cameras had caught something that was important. Looking down at the controls, I immediately became overwhelmed by the number of buttons, levers, and cranks that didn't make sense to me at all. Then again, I hadn't gotten an A in science for nothing. I pressed the replay button, and the four screens went back rapidly. Confused, I pressed stop.

My eyes froze at the picture of Spencer in a Mercedes with two men hauling a guy who looked a lot like the guy in the poster at the arcade, and that was Gerald Kruger. It had last been taken at 2:30 pm yesterday at Laden Hill!

Score!

The picture at the fourth camera showed concerned groups of people standing outside the arcade as police officers bustled in. I spotted Jolene making a phone call – the same call I'd received *after* Gerald had been reported missing. My eyes flew from one image to the other, my mind processing the details. As Gerald was being kidnapped at his home, the convention was going on until the news leaked.

I fast-forwarded the tape to today early morning *before* the GPD had been blown up. There was actually no sign of activity in Jimmy's house or the arcade. That translated to the conclusion that Jimmy might have been at their secret hideout holding the others hostage while Dina, the oddball lady, did the dirty work. Spencer had to have accompanied Jimmy.

I had everything I wanted now, but I still didn't know where the secret hideout was. As I began wandering to the door, the clanging sound continued to ring louder and louder; until I almost heard it close to two meters away from me. I squinted at the dark and concentrated on the direction of the sound.

To the left …near some desks where files had been placed and displays. Nothing seemed out of place, but still, the banging continued and this time with a lot of vitality. I crouched and began crab-walking against the wall to the desk. That's when I noticed a rectangular line cut along the metal wall.

Using my flashlight, I traced my way through the column of desks and to the small and narrow opening.

I only pressed a red button close to the frame and as usual, fog spewed out, signaling my arrival. I bit my lip, realizing that this dark and cavernous room may have been where the hostages were kept.

It felt like I was starring in a slasher movie which seemed not to have an end, or a *happy* one if you may say. Goosebumps attacked my skin, making me feel as if I was in a freezing cauldron. My flashlight began to flicker, and I felt my heart plunge in sorrow. My sneakers were clunking on the metal floor so loudly that I began tiptoeing. Who knew whether there were cameras in here as well?

I continued to wander around, wondering whether there was an end to this tunnel-like place. The banging had stopped suddenly. *Too* suddenly for me to figure out that it was definitely planned. In the brink of my hopelessness, I spotted two legs peeking out from a shelf and the muffled cry of help that the person was sending.

I went closer and stooped beside the person. Immediately I noticed the turquoise suit and the cheap-looking oxfords. "Roy? Is that you?" I asked, stunned.

He wiggled and then flipped over the surface, giving me a strained look. Roy! I untied the gag and then helped him up to his feeble feet. He looked beaten and exhausted despite his usual laid-back and bratty attitude.

"I can't believe you'd ask that, Fred. What are you doing here?" Roy asked, brushing his suit and crossing his arms.

Relieved yet shocked that Roy would still act like a jerk in the face of adversity, I grabbed his arm and began dragging him out of the room. "I don't have time to explain, Roy. Let's get out of here," I instructed him impatiently.

He firmed his arm and gave me a skeptical look. "You really think I'm going to fall for that. I've been locked up in this hideous place for a day and a half, and you just show up unexpectedly like that?" He shrugged and moved behind. "I'm not going anywhere, Fred."

"But...we're running out of time, Roy, and Gerald and a bunch of other people are in danger! Let's go!" I insisted, checking my wristwatch. "It's two o'clock. If we rush, we can make it."

"I've made myself clear, Mister," Roy growled. "I'm not..."

The door to the room groaned open, and a figure of a masculine man with bulging muscles and an enormous gait walked in, taking pride in the fact that he'd caught us now. Roy immediately gulped his words. I knew we didn't have any other option at hand; if it was one of Jimmy's men, then I knew how strong they were and how painful their punches are.

Roy clenched my shirt in a fury and asked, "Now who is that?"

"How should *I* know?" I was about to start arguing with him, but sometimes Roy can be a real pain. I turned to the man who was approaching us. "Who…are…you?" I stuttered.

I heard his knuckles cracking and his neck twisting. Wasn't that an intimidating thing wrestlers and boxers do before pummeling their opponents? Uh-oh.

"I am Jimmy McHale," he said in a baritone. "And I'm here to finish what I started."

11

The Fierce and the Fearless

My entire body began shaking, and I felt my hands and feet going numb. Jimmy looked a little – or a lot more – like an expert in kicking butt so I didn't even think a fight would settle things. As a detective, I wanted to get the facts out of him and help save Gerald Kruger not tussle with brawny Jimmy.

But Roy Watson had a *better* idea.

He caught hold of my arm and began dashing toward the rear sides of the room. For the first time, I could see the fear in Roy's eyes, and it was clear that spending a day under Jimmy's watch had really been traumatizing.

However, Jimmy knew how to play his cards right. His clunky boots bashed the floor as he lumbered after us. I knew we were in deep trouble, but we still had to save our lives.

"Why did you just do that?" I asked Roy as we ran deeper and deeper.

"Don't question me," he scoffed, making several turns in the darkness. "I've got my ways, Fred. I've stayed here for a day, so I know the routes and the lay of the land."

"Very convenient, Roy," I teased him as I huffed. My chest felt shrunken, and my head was killing me; sure signs of how stressed-out I was. I was just glad I'd found Roy…alive. "So, what was the pass card for, Roy?" I asked, seizing the moment to get answers.

Behind me, I could feel Jimmy's track clothes making noises as he rapidly moved, taking deep breaths and cursing silently. I remembered Danson telling me that he'd really changed after losing his job – had he meant mentally too?

"I thought it would be better if I gave it to you than for someone to stumble upon it and come to know of this place," Roy said, sighing spasmodically. "PR managers always get those cards for them to access the facilities."

"I don't understand," I said, trying to ignore Jimmy's rapid breathing behind me. "Why did you tell me it was an invite if it really isn't?"

"You're the most curious kid I've ever met. And that's not very pleasing. I figured if I told you it was an invite you'd not get all crazy with questions," Roy admitted, sounding guilty. I had to admit he was true about me being curious. "And Gerald had told me that pass card would be very useful in keeping his matters confidential. You and I know I'm not good with secrets."

"So you gave me the pass card to evade responsibility," I summed up with a skeptical tone.

"Yeah, that," Roy said. He began sounding bellicose. "I wish I hadn't."

"Why?" I became tangled in confusion again.

"Because I was kidnapped later. And illegally held hostage in this lair by that guy Jimmy," Roy said, agitated. "I think he wanted that pass card really badly. What's his deal anyway?"

"That's what I'm going to find out," I told him with finality.

We continue running through the winding hallways, Roy leading me as I kept watch of Jimmy. After some minutes of trial and error around the tunnels, we stopped at a door which didn't barge when I tried unlocking it. I could see Jimmy's shadowy figure hovering towards us.

"You're mine now!" Jimmy roared, reaching for a hard-metallic object from his leather jacket pocket. It looked like a revolver – a killer revolver.

Roy gave me a frantic look then sighed and shook his head. "Fine Jimmy, you caught us. But what's the matter with you? You're acting like some psycho," he said in a daring voice. That's Roy Watson for you.

"He got his revenge, and now he wants to 'dispose us'" I told Roy, giving Jimmy a glance of surprise. "Isn't that so?"

Jimmy's face contorted in mild surprise. "How did you know that?" he asked, still clenching his gun and grinding his teeth in rage.

He looked like a time bomb, to be frank.

"I overheard a certain Spencer, the guy who almost got killed on the front porch of *your* house, having a conversation with you and surprisingly *you* want to kill us, take the money and fly away by *yourself*," I said, waiting for Jimmy to react. "Don't you think that's a little bit selfish of you?"

"Correction; Spencer is gone. And so, will you two, after I deal with you," Jimmy shot back aggressively.

"Where are you holding the others?" I asked Jimmy, feeling sad that we'd lost one suspect. "Why did you kill your wingman? And what exactly do you want from us?"

"See, that's the kind of attitude I hate about you," Jimmy said, brandishing the gun firmly in his gnarly hands. "I'll tell you anyway because you're all coming to an end and I won't have to deal with the cops anymore. Firstly, this is a secret facility which is owned by Gerald Kruger. It's nice and all, pretty good for locking guys up and watching the backs of the cops and you."

I got a tingle down my spine. Did he mean he'd been watching us all this time? "A facility all the way here? Doesn't seem very convenient after all," I said, rolling my eyes.

Jimmy narrowed his eyes. "Gerald Kruger and I didn't really start off on a good note," he mumbled.

"Just because he refused to admit you to his company for the internship? That sounds juvenile," I said.

"Juvenile? I needed that internship job! Look at where I live…in the middle of abject poverty, and you call it juvenile?" He was uncontrollably bobbing in anger. "I don't know why, but I lived with that pain for so long, and during that period, I planned on how to get my revenge."

"Is that why you kidnapped Gerald and then snuck in Greens Association's equipment to his apartment?" I asked.

Jimmy nodded grudgingly. "I used to work in GA, and that's how I came to know you. I lost my internship job to you. I failed to land a spot in Tech World. Furious, I decided I had to sabotage Gerald so when his convention came to Glades I saw the golden opportunity and planted the equipment in his apartment." He tweaked his eyes in contempt. "Then you and your two friends showed up. I decided that I had to take care of you three for being nosy and making me lose a job while Gerald was paying for it."

I had to admit this guy really sounded like a psycho.

"How am *I* involved? I'm not one of Fred's friends," Roy smugly said, giving me a glance of disdain.

"Well, you were Gerald's PR…and whoever is Gerald's associate is an enemy of mine," he said, chuckling. "And I still needed the pass card to open up this place. I know it because he set his lair under my house. What a giveaway it was for me when I kidnapped you, but then you told me *Fred* had it. So, I used the back route and hid you in the room through the back door instead of using the locked door." He turned his glower at me. "Then I did all I could to spook you and get it. Instead, I got you."

"The fire, why would you plan to kill Officer Timmons?" I asked.

His expression turned to a dreamy one. "My girlfriend had that score settled. Dina, she works at Hangout, and that day when I saw you there I knew you were on to me," he said. "Luckily, my plan worked. I threw the cops off the scent since I had their boss under my dominion. All my plans worked."

"And why would you murder your own wingman, Spencer?" I pressed.

Jimmy gave me a stone-cold look. "Spencer also lost his job at Tech World and was on the same mission as I was. Our paths crossed and we began working together to finish Gerald. He then grew all too demanding, so after all that trouble he went through I decided that I had to remove him from the big picture."

"And what exactly *is* the big picture?" Roy chimed in.

"Getting Gerald's money, kill him and the hostages and then fly with Dina to Hawaii for summer vacation," he proudly professed.

"Some picture," Roy muttered.

After all the confession, I could not believe Jimmy's motive had just been revenge and greed. He had stooped low – too low and now he wanted to kill us. I really felt the kind of trauma his younger brother felt when he acted up his tantrums concerning poverty. But now that he'd gotten all that he wanted, I felt like it was now our turn to stage an escape.

I just hoped Roy was thinking the same thing as Jimmy cocked his gun. I hadn't come this close to a gun, so all my blood turned cold and my face went pale. Were the police shrewd enough to explore the deep parts of this tunnel and find us, or were we headed for disaster?

"Well, say your last prayers meddlers because this will be the last summer you will ever live to see," Jimmy said, his threat making my insides flip over.

I glanced behind Jimmy to the long tunnel we'd passed, wishing the police would arrive fast. Jimmy had probably not gone to his other secret hideout, so if we jumped him, he'd still kill Officer T and Gerald. I gave Roy a signal: Run to the side.

He gave me a *what, you dork* look and then nodded slowly as I pointed to Jimmy's side. The good news was that he was busy loading his gun, but the bad news was that he was too big so we couldn't make it past the sides.

But the worst news was that before I could abort that plan, Roy had already taken off. I watched in horror as Roy ducked a close-range bullet clearly meant for his head.

"Run!" I yelled at him, darting to another exit to my left. I knew perfectly well Jimmy couldn't manage shooting two people at once; – especially if they were headed to different directions.

I didn't know where I was headed, but it didn't look familiar. I couldn't see Jimmy, but I could hear bullets sounding everywhere. I wound up in a closed door which readily slid to the sides with help from the pass card. If Roy hadn't deliberately used me to evade his responsibility, I don't know how I would have fared on. The door led to a lot of winding hallways until I got to another slightly ajar door from where I could see Jay, still standing beside the cans. The store room.

Yes! I dug my way past the pile of equipment and then pushed the back door open in spite of the cans proving to be hard to move. I mean, how long had they stayed lodged there? Feeling a wave of relief washing over me, I breathed in the fresh air and threw an embrace over Jay.

"Man, how long did you stay in there? I was beginning to think you got caught or something," Jay said, the red ruddy color of his face returning.

"Long enough for me to crack the case. But we need to find Roy...he ran away when Jimmy began firing," I told Jay, looking inside the door. It still seemed creepy and dark in there. "I can't imagine Gerald built a lair in such a place."

"Huh?" Jay asked.

"I'll explain later," I told him, suddenly feeling some movement in the store room. Jay and I peeked inside, and I saw an arm emerging. "Is that you, Roy?" I called out, shoving away the cans and pulling the door wider.

"Yes. And pull me out now!" He demanded as his torso emerged from the mountain of equipment stashed in the store.

"Even when in danger he's still the jerk we can't live without, huh?" Jay teased as he copped hold of Roy's shoulders and gave him a boost out. He gave him a hug, Roy resisting and frowning indignantly. "I still don't like you, Roy. So, don't get me wrong," Jay said, shoving the door back.

After pulling himself away from Jay, Roy, still disgruntled, said, "I'm barely glad to see you too." He turned to me, and his mouth became a taut line. "You really had the nerve to leave me back there with that psychopath Jimmy?

I'm not forgiving you for that, Fred."

I knew better than to argue so I kept my lips sealed.

"You should be happy he saved you," Jay protested. "Or else we'd still be roaming around Glades looking for you."

I stole a glance at my watch and grimaced. "We still have time to look for the other hostages…" My words drained away when I saw a familiar nozzle of a revolver, Jimmy's revolver, planted on my neck. Jay and Roy gasped and moved back, bumping into the two allies of Jimmy. "I guess not," I whispered weakly.

Jimmy's snigger made me feel like puking. How had he made it outside without drawing too much attention to himself? I spun around and caught the proud glimmer in his eyes and the weary look on his parched face.

"You're going with *me*," he ordered, and he led us into a Mercedes parked behind his ramshackle of a house.

Roy gave me a demeaning once-over and sighed, "If we get out alive, I'm going to seriously grind you to dust!"

12

Blast Off

Jimmy's men shoved us into the backseat of the car and strapped us with duct tape to the seats. It felt like we'd repeated this scenario too many times; the bad guy shows up, we get into trouble with him and then perhaps some good luck rolls up our way.

But now it felt as though the situation was growing bleaker by the minute. As Jimmy eased into his seat, I was itching to ask him how he'd got out of the lair but I figured he knew his way through it since he lived above it. The place was suddenly as deserted as it had been when we arrived, except for the group of men we had found outside Jimmy's house.

"You know those guys?" I asked Roy, keeping my voice to a whisper.

Roy looked out then shrugged and said, "That man there, on the hammock, is a prophet. Calls himself Roger. He saw me being dragged here and gave me a creepy look as if he knew I was in serious trouble." He nodded at Roger who was plopped by a tree. "See, that kind of look."

I felt a shiver down my back as he gave us a look of sorrow. Roger seemed good at the prophesying thing; maybe he'd known that Spencer would be killed and we'd be trapped by Jimmy.

"Shut up back there!" Jimmy said with a sneer. "If you knew what's good for you, you'd be quiet."

Jay nudged me from his seat and whispered, "Is Jimmy really the culprit,?"

I nodded, glancing at the sneer on Jimmy's face as he swerved the car away from a speeding truck and onto the street adjacent to Triton. I had every reason to believe the police had given up on their search, and everyone had gone back home with no hope of ever finding Jimmy; or Spencer since he was cold dead.

"So, where are we going?" Jay asked out aloud.

Jimmy grunted uncomfortably. He plainly didn't like that question. Obviously, not every serial kidnapper with a consort of heavy and robust guys would answer that with a sense of comfort.

"Don't worry about that," Jimmy shot back. "Just remain quiet, and don't even try screaming or making a stupid scene."

This guy was out of his mind. He acted so tough and hardcore; but I could see the fear in his eyes, his shaking hands making an attempt to grip the wheel, and his neck veins bulging out in anger. I wanted to scream, yes. But who would think we were in a grim mess? Jimmy wouldn't stop even if pedestrians began throwing stones and flinging shoes because he had held hostage three innocent kids.

Phone! I would alert the police and let them know that Jimmy was roaming around the northern area of Glades with us in a Mercedes. Hmmm, probably Spencer's Mercedes. My mind flew to Jolene; had she amassed anything extra about Jimmy, and did she perceive we were in trouble?

On cue, 'Rock It All' by Fred Guzzle, Yes, I liked his music; began ringing through my phone. Sandwiched between Jay and one of the huge men and my phone in my right pocket, it was difficult to reach it. And Jimmy had been very dumb to forget to cuff us. Maybe he was a dork as Jolene had said.

"Bring me that phone!" Jimmy barked with a gruff voice.

I glanced at the screen and bit my lip. "But it's my mom. She's probably sick to the gut about my whereabouts."

"It's only three in the afternoon," Jimmy protested, his eyes fixed on the road. We were deep in the city center by now. "Give it to me now. I have no time to waste."

Reluctantly, I handed my phone to him. Would he crash it just like he'd done to the GA equipment? Which made me ask why he'd done that; and all he said was, "To get my revenge on Mr. Green, or did he change his name to Brown?"

"What are you gonna tell her?" I asked Jimmy.

"The same thing I told Roy's parents: their son is with me, and I demand ransom," Jimmy conceded with an evil grin which didn't last. "Would you shut up? ? I have to get to Marino Grounds and get through with this."

"Marino Grounds?" Jay, Roy, and I all repeated; my eyes widening.

Jimmy banged the wheel in a fury and snapped his tongue. "I was hoping to make it top-secret and private," he said, gritting his teeth.

See? Not the smartest culprit Glades has ever had.

"We'll just tell the police," Roy said with a confident smile which also didn't last. "*After* we get our phones and check for emails. Some of us are trying to build a career as PR agents for super-famous scientists."

"You're already guilty of almost everything that has been happening, Jimmy. Why don't you just throw in the towel and drop by the jail?" I asked sarcastically.

Jimmy winced a little but recovered fast and shot us a smirk. "Make me, dweebs."

Which criminal says that?

Just as it was starting to get hotter than eighty-five degrees, Jimmy drove away from the bustling city center and into the darker and inhabitable parts of Glades; The Jitters. It's named that way because this part of Glades was once a very productive irrigation scheme which was surrounded by fields of glades, and from which we named the town. Now, the story is a bit different because due to weather changes and industrialization, the scheme broke down and trees crept up and blossomed, hiding the beautiful glades that brought pride to the town.

Um, you may wonder how I know all that...but when I'm nervous, I tend to blabber anything.

So, after all that change, the place became sort of scary and gave people jitters just thinking about it. And *I* was not an exception.

"Why would Gerald host the convention in such a murky and disgusting place?" Roy asked, clearly irked. "I'm starting to re-think this whole PR thing."

"You should," Jimmy said with a blunt tone. He began riding along a deserted track that was flanked by thickets and overgrown bushes. As we rode deeper and deeper, the sun dimmed out, and the luminescence from the car's lights was the only resort to seeing in front. Jimmy began chuckling and glanced behind. "Are you scared?" he asked in a mocking voice.

"Not if *you* are," Jay replied with an equal mocking voice.

One of Jimmy's men stirred in his seat and removed what looked like a piece of cotton cloth. He dipped a slurp of liquid on it from a small tub in his pocket, and before any one of us knew it, Jay was knocked out!

Knowing that any other silly remark would make me end up like Jay, with eyes shut and face drooping, I decided to let Jimmy have his way. He was really good at talking trash but maybe not so good when it came to being subtle. I had a premonition the cops were on their way. I hoped that premonition would last.

"That ought to shut your mouths up. And teach you never to meddle with Jimmy McHale and his elaborate plans," Jimmy snickered loudly, his men joining in.

I rolled my eyes furtively. I wouldn't really call his plans 'elaborate'; more like warped-out plans by a deadbeat junkie. Jimmy rode down the road until we got to a clearing. Far in the distant, I saw a chopper getting ready to land, its rotor blades slicing through the air like knives. It suddenly began feeling like zero degrees.

"Great job, men. The chopper's already here," Jimmy said lowly, his grin widening into a sneer. "Now here is where it gets more fun." He skidded to a stop near the chopper, scrambled out, and ordered his men to pull us out and throw us into the awaiting chopper.

The pilot inside the chopper licked his dry, chapped lips with glee, looking at us like we were tiny little chicks in a battlefield full of hawks.

The men gagged us forcefully, hoisted us up by the retractable rubber rungs that were in the small space inside the chopper. Glancing around with my hawk-eyed senses, I saw three large shiny suitcases gleaming from the back placed side by side with some cartons with the logo Tech World stenciled on each of them.

Jimmy had plundered some of the equipment!

As soon as we were settled in, Jimmy clambered up; followed by his two assistants. He held my head up and whispered in a hush, "How do you like it now, Fred? I lost my job because of you, and now you're gonna lose your life! What do you value more, a job or your life?"

His pungent smell made me think twice about that question. Maybe I wanted *fresh air*! The pilot did a swift test of the plane's controls and pre-checked the levers and gears. At least that's what he told Jimmy when he asked. I doubted him, though.

Jay's body was jammed between Roy and me at the back with the two men sitting beside Jimmy in the front seat. I just wished that I'd see where we were headed as the chopper began to jerk forward.

Jimmy murmured with the two men, chuckled, and then he turned to me with a deep frown. "Let's see whether you'll get yourself out of this one, Fred," he growled and reclined back on his seat.

Yeah, let us see.

13

The Birth of Detective Fred

I felt the chopper rising and the rotor blades whirling at a fast speed. The pilot steered the chopper away from the clearing and began directing it headed to the forest area, clearly getting away from Marino Grounds as fast as he could manage. What about the other hostages? Had he already killed them?

I shifted myself to the nearest window and peered out. Jimmy and his goons were yapping away about their success and how top-hole their plans had been, but I didn't focus on them. The chopper was now a few feet away from the ground, tumbling in imbalance before it gained speed steadily.

My eyes searched the silent grounds where the convention was intended to be held, the rolling plains, the dark forest, and the topographical view of Glades as the chopper went higher and higher.

Where were the cops? I was beginning to feel torpid and airsick maybe from thinking that this was going to be the end of my sixteenth life on earth.

The pilot spoke up with a shaky voice.

"Um...Jimmy...the men in blue are onto us!"

I shot Roy a triumphant look which he obviously dodged and rolled his eyes.

I knew he had a grudge with me, but that was the most trivial thing that was on my mind now. The police had finally tracked us down.

Jimmy sputtered angrily, "What? I... I thought we'd downright lost them t. Okay, move over Danny. I'm taking the wheel."

Danny, the pilot with prickly stubble and goggles, shook his head adamantly and frowned. "Hey! You promised to pay me a hundred big ones if I did this on my own. There's no way I'm losing such money consciously."

"Just move Danny," Jimmy ordered and eased to the cockpit, pushing Danny aside and gripping the lever. "If the cops wanna showdown, I'll give them a smack down."

Jimmy's men lugged Danny out of the cockpit and squeezed him between themselves. Though he was still grouching, Danny crossed his arms and silently watched as Jimmy maneuvered his way from the forest and made a turn back to the grounds.

"What are you doing, Jimmy? We're supposed to be leaving for the airport," one of the men said, leaning forward. His finger pointed to the left window "And it's *that* way. You're going the wrong way."

"Are you breaching the plan?" the other guy said with a scratchy tone.

Jimmy shrugged and brought the chopper above the squad cars below.

He paused for a minute, his eyes roaming over the panel. "Um, Danny, how do I move down? These levers are way too confusing."

Wow! Very professional.

Danny, looking as if he wanted to cop out of telling him, laughed languidly. "I thought you wanted a show down with the cops by yourself," he said with a curt chuckle. "I don't want to pester you, boss. Do your thing."

One of the men firmed his grip on Danny's neck and breathed, "Don't be a smart guy here."

As they grappled amongst themselves, I already had my penknife with me, and I was figuring out a way to cut the cords wrapped around my hands. Roy, seemingly bored, gave me an impassive look then narrowed his eyes at me. Perhaps he was thinking how selfish I was by saving myself first, but the truth is that I wanted to make our escape as subtle as possible. If I tore open Roy's gag, he'd begin blubbering all over again, and we'd be in hotter soup.

I began cutting the sisal cords, but the penknife wasn't equal to the task and only grazed the cord. Roy shot me an impatient look and nodded at the cockpit. Jimmy was still arguing with Danny on who got to ride the chopper, so that bought us time to cut the cords successfully using an electronic laser cutter Roy had stumbled upon in Gerald's lair.

At long last Roy and I were free of our gags and cords. I stooped beside Jay who was now coming around and began burning across the cords with the beam.

But luck wasn't on our side. My penknife accidentally slid from my pocket, and before I could lunge for it, it fell on the floor, making a clinking sound which made Jimmy, Danny, and the two men look behind in one swift move.

"Look what *you* did!" Roy cried, shooting me a perfunctory smirk as if he wasn't in the same danger as I was. "Fred, you're a killjoy! Now the bad guys are seriously pissed off, and they should tie you again and let me go." He ran his hand through his hair and smoothed down his now-creased suit.

'Oh yeah. As if trying to please the bad guys was going to save his sorry rear-end.' Even I could act flamboyantly in front of the bad guys, they would still have my sorry rear-end tied up again.

Jimmy's jaw dropped in amazement, but now it seemed his biggest issue was to control the chopper. "Danny, get back to the wheel. I've got some bait to feed," he hissed. His trademark disturbing chuckle followed.

As he jumped over the seat, out of nowhere, Danny lunged forward and toppled Jimmy down. They rolled a few times on the floor, banging their knees against the metal boxes and bashing their heads on the sides of the chopper. Surprisingly, Danny had turned against his boss, and he seriously looked as if he had *never* been on his side.

Jimmy's men scrambled from their seats and grabbed Danny from the floor as Jimmy removed his revolver from his pocket.

Jay sat up and rubbed his head severally, looking around with a blank stare. Glad that he was conscious but confused about what was happening, he tapped my leg and pointed weakly at the cockpit.

"The controls!" I gasped, realizing that there was no one to control the chopper.

Before I could thank Jay, I was already headed for the cockpit. Jimmy's men were preoccupied with pinning Danny down, Jimmy boring a gun down the poor guy's throat, so I was clear.

The chopper's controls looked complicated with all the flickering lights, the switches, and the cranks. How was I going to safely get us all down without even an ounce of aviation knowledge? I didn't even like being a pilot let alone *fly a plane*.

"Fred, step away from the cockpit," I heard Jimmy's sonorous voice slice through the whirring sound of the air rushing forward. Oh no! We were going to die!

I turned back and met the revolver's nozzle pointed at my nose.

This guy was proving to be a thick-headed person but also a very witty dude; booby traps, using frags, and bombing the GPD using lithium bombs...who knew what he could do with that revolver?

I know, stick it into my nose and pull the trigger!

"We all know that's way too risky," I said, the chopper beginning to nosedive. The metal boxes began edging away from the wall as the momentum thrust us down with great velocity. "We might die, Jimmy!"

"That's what I want, kid. Now step away, and let go of that lever NOW!" He sounded edgy, but a little bit scared for an intrepid troublemaker.

My eyes moved from the revolver, to Jimmy's men who were dealing with Danny, and to the ground below which was now becoming clearer. I checked the speedometer gauge, and my eyes nearly popped out due to shock. A chopper plummeting towards the earth at five hundred mph isn't anyone's regular piece of cake.

"Move over!" Jimmy didn't relent from giving commands.

My heart was now literally pumping. The chopper was going to crash, and we were going to die. Didn't sound like a very good thing to say let alone think about it. Then I noticed, out of the corner of my eye, the metal boxes moving closer and closer.

Inertia. I had to admit school had really come to be of great use.

The revolver clicked, Jimmy's finger moved to the trigger, and then I waited for the right moment before the metal boxes came tumbling down, and I yanked the lever up instinctively.

Jimmy was flung to the side, knocked his head against the metal floor, and his eyes rolled up. Out. His men, like blind rats after cheese, knocked down the door and took an unexpected leap.

"Now *that* is epic!" I said, laughing. I turned to Roy and Jay who were staring at the open door in utter shock and winked at both of them.

"Not gonna happen, Fred," Roy smirked. "Just get me outta here."

I managed to steady the chopper, found a clear spot to land it without the chopper having to plow its way through the trees, and finally roll down the glades and go up in flames. Sheesh.

The minute the chopper touched down, Jolene, two police officer's I didn't know, and Mr. Green came to the door, wrenched it open, and we were led out of the chopper.

"Oops," Jay whispered to me, pointing at Mr. Green who wore a stony look on his face. "Boss is here. What do you think he's gonna say about us?"

"Don't worry," I assured Jay, ignoring the looks we got from other onlookers as if we had come from the dead. Glades never gets as much suspense and thrill as you can get when you ride a roller coaster ten times constantly, so you'd understand why they were busy cupping their mouths and making gasping sounds.

Dylan walked towards us, holding his iPod up, and looking concerned. He was accompanied by Jay's, Roy's, and my parents, trailing him and wearing forlorn looks. *My* parents actually were always worry bugs. And Officer Timmons together with a tall, tanned man. Perhaps Gerald Kruger.

Oh...and a thin, wiry redhead stalking behind them – Dart Preston.

"It's like a reunion," he cried once he reached our side and put the microphone under my mouth. "Fred Turner, blockbuster kid, crackpot genius, detective, or maybe a Soviet spy...let him tell it."

I stared at the camera like some hypnotized freak with Dart flashing me a smile and the cameraman giving me a *Talk already* look. What was I going to say, that Jimmy, a guy after revenge for failing to miss a job opportunity, and being booted out from an internship job, had almost killed us; and flown to Hawaii for a vacation without an ounce of guilt? And now that his consort had been shredded to bits of human meat chunks by the chopper's propeller and his accomplice had been blown to death, he, is freaky pilot and his princess Dina was the only ones to serve jail term?

Um, actually that's what I told Dart, without any hard feelings about his nutty behavior and happy-go-lucky attitude of a reporter. At least I was relieved to be safe.

As the police officers dragged Jimmy, Dina, and Danny away into an awaiting squad car, my parents and I exchanged bear hugs. They'd heard me explaining to Dart and the entire USA about Jimmy and looked proud and impressed.

"You *can* be a detective for all I care, son," Dad said, patting my head. "I just wish next time you won't be risking your life riding a chopper for the sake of justice."

"That's right, Fred," Mom agreed, hugging me tightly.

Jay waited for me to finish up with my parents and pulled me away to Mr. Green and Gerald who were standing with Officer Timmons not far from the seized chopper.

"I just can't bring myself to think that you, Fred, helped save Gerald here," Mr. Green spoke up, his chest puffing with delight. He pushed his glasses up his nose. "And also, saving our companies from bad publicity. I just cannot believe it."

"Well you better," I said. I turned to Gerald. He looked impassive but thankful.

"Gerald, it's a pleasure to meet you in person. My name's Fred Turner," I said, extending my hand to shake his smooth and moist hand. "I'm the guy who's been sweating day and night to find you. No doubt I'm relieved."

"Words cannot express my gratitude to you, Turner," Gerald said with an exquisite accent. "I'm just so glad that I'm no longer a hostage held in a cellar under Marino Grounds Hotel. That's where the convention I had planned for was supposed to be held." His eyes stared down at his feet. "Guess now all my money and hard work has gone to waste because of a guy who couldn't take no for an answer."

Jay laughed. "Petty, isn't it?"

I fished out the pass card and handed it to Gerald. "This belongs to you, Gerald. The key to your lair ," I said as he examined the card. "Your PR agent gave it to me because..."

"Because I was out of my mind," Roy blurted, pushing me aside and shaking Gerald's hand heartily. "And I quit!"

Before any of us could stop him, he flounced away with his messed-up suit and straggly hair. After being locked in a lair, almost killed in a chopper crash, and quitting his job; he really needed a rest more than any of us did.

"Wow! I mean, thank you a lot. I'm kinda thinking of moving the location of my lair to somewhere more secret. That's kinda how Jimmy found out where to steal my money, right?" Gerald smiled sympathetically at himself.

"Don't worry buddy. At least Fred here caught him before he flew off with the money," Mr. Green said, punching his friend on the arm. He turned to me and gave me a sincerely cordial look. "Thank you again. You've proved to be more than just a clean-up fag."

"And me?" Jay put in with a skeptical look.

"Well, I'm willing to promote both of you to clerical assistants!" Mr. Green said, waving his hands in a dramatic flair.

"Good job, boys. I'm proud of you," Officer Timmons said plainly; and walked away with the two businessmen sharing jokes.

Jolene walked by, with Danson holding her hand and supporting his other with a crutch. Looks like he'd been roughed up by Jimmy's men but seemed to have let it go. "Congrats, Jay! Now you don't have to mop the floor with your soggy and overgrown hair anymore," she teased, flipping back her hair. She turned to Danson and smiled at him. "See, Danny, I know how to tease."

Jay chuckled good-naturedly, and the four of us began walking back to my car parked just along the dirt track that had been brought by Jolene.

That evening, I didn't know what was odd. Maybe it was because Jolene had made up with Danson, who had been held hostage by his evil brother. Or maybe it's because Danson hadn't found a nickname for Jolene. I could also say it was because I came to save the convention which I hadn't been invited initially.

But because Gerald had decided to host the convention again after all, with yours truly one hundred percent invited, and I was going to report to work Monday as a clerical assistant, maybe it wasn't *that* all odd.

Jay caught up with me and smiled. "Maybe this isn't the worst day of our lives after all. Am I right, Detective Fred?"

All I could do was smile back.

Catch a glimpse of Fred's case...

There is a new scientist in Glades town, and Fred, Jay, and Jolene can't wait to attend the convention that is being held to honor the renowned scientist, Mr. Gerald Kruger. The Bad news is that Fred doesn't get to go since he hasn't been invited. But that isn't such a big deal when things start going haywire.

Especially because death threats, dangerous booby traps, life-threatening incidences and weird friendly nemeses just don't happen naturally.

A few more victims and it becomes weird. It doesn't take rocket science for Fred, Jay, and Jolene to realize that *they* are also in the line of danger. Fred has to stop all this before the mastermind strikes a deathly blow once again In...